Skelton Yorke

Aunt Margaret's little neighbours

or Chats about the rosary

Skelton Yorke

Aunt Margaret's little neighbours
or Chats about the rosary

ISBN/EAN: 9783742860293

Manufactured in Europe, USA, Canada, Australia, Japa

Cover: Foto ©Andreas Hilbeck / pixelio.de

Manufactured and distributed by brebook publishing software
(www.brebook.com)

Skelton Yorke

Aunt Margaret's little neighbours

AUNT MARGARET'S LITTLE NEIGHBOURS;

OR,

CHATS ABOUT THE ROSARY.

BY

SKELTON YORKE,

AUTHOR OF "HILDA."

LONDON:

R. WASHBOURNE, 18A, PATERNOSTER ROW.

1872.

CONTENTS.

AUNT MARGARET'S LITTLE NEIGHBOURS.

STORY OF THE FIRST BEAD.

HUMILITY.

IN a certain little class-room, on a dull October evening, a number of children were assembled. A bright fire burned, and a gas-light made the room very cheerful, and the children listened to the rain now beginning to patter against the window panes, and were glad of the light and the warmth.

There were fifteen of these children, and they varied greatly in age and appearance. The eldest and the youngest were the Doctor's children, and the Doctor was Aunt Margaret's brother, so my little friends may guess what relation Harry and Christine were to Aunt Margaret. Harry was a sickly boy of fifteen, marked by disease for an early grave, and if the rain had begun to fall earlier he would

1

not have been allowed to go out that evening.
Christine was only seven, a gay, happy, butterfly-
kind of child, bright and pretty and loving, and
devoted to play.

Christine's fair curls and sparkling blue eyes con-
trasted strangely with the heavy countenance and
dark complexion of her neighbour, Katy McGraith,
who sat next her, and was only one year older.
Christine had had many more advantages than
Katy, her daily reading lesson was conned at her
mother's knee, and every one, papa, mamma, aunt,
and Harry were giving her good advice and good
example at every opportunity. But Katy had to
nurse the baby when at home, and to plod through
rain and mud to school, and was often so cold and
hungry and wet that learning seemed doubly difficult, but small Katy had a resolute will, and she
had a great motive for "getting on with her book."
Katy like Christine had a big brother, and there he
sat beside Harry, but what a contrast in the appearance of the two ! Harry so fair and delicate
looking, and Jack burly and with blackened face.
Jack seemed to understand everything by means of
Katy's intelligence. He worked in the coal-mine
all day, and when he came home for his supper he
made Katy sit on his knee and teach him his lesson
for " the Lady's" next class, for poor Jack had had

no chance of learning to read, no school having been opened in that district till his working days had begun.

And then there was Minnie McGraith, older and more sunny-looking than Katy, but she was already out in place, having reached her eleventh year; but by diligence during the day she earned the favour of an occasional evening in the class-room. Johnny O'Rourke was also a little coal-worker, but his blackened face could not conceal the merry twinkle of his eyes; he sat beside Jack McGraith, and his sister Polly was beside him, a girl as big and old as Harry, but very ignorant, because she had gone to work at the tin manufactory before the school was built or spoken of.

And there was Tom and Eleanor Morris, the draper's children; and thoughtful Ethel Rivers, with her twin little sisters Nora and Julia; and widow Sullivan's trio, Ellen and Jane, and little Pat. All these children lived near to Aunt Margaret, and she could easily collect them for evening classes, and monthly meetings, and whatever else she wanted them for, as they were always glad of the chance of spending an hour with her.

On the present occasion she had brought them together to form what is called a circle of the Living Rosary. Harry was the only one who understood what it meant, and Jack, and Johnny, and Minnie, and Katy had come meaning to learn to understand it. The rest had come because Aunt Margaret had called them, and they had a notion that somehow or other their souls would be better for coming.

They sat around her table, making a real circle there; each had a Rosary in the hand, and each looked curiously at a great big Rosary that lay on the table. Moreover Aunt Margaret had given to each a picture, and now that they were waiting while she was detained in the school, they glanced from Rosary to picture, and from picture to Rosary, and didn't know what to make of it.

"I've got a pretty lady on my picture," said Christine, who could never keep silence for five minutes at a time, "and a nice boy, with wings on, is giving her a flower. What have you got, Katy?"

"She do call it a pretty lady, and it be the Blessed Virgin!" exclaimed Minnie, in her rough downright way, for she had seen the picture before.

"Oh, its the Blessed Virgin, is it?" said Christine; "well, but she is a lady too, 'Our Lady,' mamma calls her. And I do believe the other is an angel. It's a nice picture, how I wish there was a story about it, don't you, Harry?"

"There is a story," said a clear voice, and the

children started, and looked full of curiosity for the voice really seemed to come from the big Rosary on the table. There was a silence for some time, and Christine blushed with eagerness, and then the voice spoke again.

" Be very quiet, children, and listen to me. Take the first large bead on your Rosaries in your hand, and you shall hear a wonderful story."

They did as the voice desired, and listened with breathless eagerness, and it spoke as follows :

" There was a beautiful land which belonged to a great and good man, and he was the King of it. There were houses and gardens, fields and woods ; rivers and valleys, trees of all kinds, and plenty of cattle ; and there was no one to enjoy this good land. The King was a very great King, for he had a still finer land than that, and it had many people in it, but even it could hold far more. So the King said he would bring some men and women and children to the new land, and they should live and serve him there ; and they who did well to the land that he first gave them should be rewarded by still better homes in the best land of all.

" First he put only one man and woman into the new country, and he gave them a good garden and orchard, and they had nothing to do but to keep it in order. They had everything for their own, except one tree, and that they were not to touch.

" Now a long way off there was another king as bad as our King was good. He used to be an officer in our King's army, but he rebelled, and gave himself up to his own pride, and was turned out of the good land, and sent down, down into a black country underground, where the sun never shines, and the birds never sing, but where it is dark and hot and full of bad smells, and never a flower to be seen. So the rebel said, 'Never mind, I had rather be a king here than a slave up yonder, and I will not stop alone in this prison, but I will draw lots of the King's subjects hither, and rob his fine land on every side.' So the Robber-king lived in his stifling dungeons, and watched what harm he could do to the good King.

" And as he wandered about one day he saw the people at work in their new garden, and he was jealous, and said, ' Ah, the King will get new subjects here, everyone with a heart to love him, and the sight of their happiness will make him glad ! I will steal them for my dungeons, and then he will bite his tongue for rage.'

" But the Robber could not steal the man and woman, for though he approached ever so near to them, there was ever a bright creature at the side of each, protecting them from danger, and it was the Rebel-king who had to bite his tongue for rage. But still he watched, and watched.

"And as he watched, he saw that the man and the woman had each a jewel in the heart, a jewel like a bright light, and it burned upwards towards the throne of the good King, and he read words written under the jewelled light, 'To love is to obey. Who loves me I will keep from all danger.' So the Robber knew that if he could steal that jewel, the guardian angel would no longer have power to protect.

"'To love is to obey.' The more he thought about this, the more cruel and clever he became, and at last he got the people to take fruit from the forbidden tree, and then the jewelled lights turned towards him, and he could take them from the disobedient hearts. And he was glad, and went back to his stifling dungeons to make ready a place for the new people whom he would presently fetch thither; and he and his fellow-robbers rejoiced, because they thought they had destroyed the work of the good King.

"When it was known in the good land that the King's new people had turned from him, all were silent and sad. But the King's son spoke presently, and he said, 'It is just, O my royal father, that those who rebel against thee, should die as traitors, but I pity and love these poor creatures, and so I will die instead of them.'

"The King loved his beautiful son more than ever he had done before when he heard these noble words, and he said that loving offer was worthy the great heart of a royal prince, but, he added, it must be one of the very people that had rebelled that must die to satisfy justice, but where could one be found so good and great as to be worth all the people who should ever spring from those parents, for now all their children would be born with black rebellious hearts.

"And the King's son spoke again, and he said, ' I will do it all myself. I will become a little baby, the child of one of the daughters of these people. I being of one blood with thee, my royal father, am worth all the people that can ever be born as slaves of the vile robber. When a maiden with a clean heart can be found, I will go to her, and be her child, and I will live among the people in the new country, and die for their fault, and teach them how to win a right to the possessions thou hast prepared for them in this good land where all is gladness and joy.'

"Then all the white guards in the palace sang joyfully, and praised the good and generous prince, who so loved his poor outlawed creatures, and from that time they called him the Prince of Peace.

"The good King then went down to the disobedient creatures who were crouching behind the bushes in fear of his just anger, for they knew that they deserved death. He told them that they must have died then and there, but that a new hope had arisen for them, for that in due time one should be born of a daughter of theirs, who should pay all their debts, and buy back their homes in the good land for them; but that, in the meanwhile, they must endure sorrow and pain, for the Robber-king had now got a key to their hearts, and would always be stealing their jewels, only if they really tried to defend them, and keep them burning towards the good King, the white guards should come unseen and help them in the fight, and even fetch the jewels back for them when they should sincerely mourn their loss. And then the King went away, for he could no more walk in the new country now that rebellion had begun there, only his guards would go to help the poor persecuted creatures to make head against the robbers.

"And so that man and woman lived, and fought, and laboured, and they had children, and grandchildren, and great-grandchildren, and the new country grew full of people, and every day, and everywhere, the black robbers were busy stealing the jewels, and dragging the people to their horrid dungeons. And the white guards were busy too, reminding the people to grieve for their lost jewels, and call upon the Prince of Peace, and so get them back again, at which the robbers howled with vexation.

"And the old people fulfilled their time in the working country, and might have gone to their bright homes in the Good Land, but that the gates were now locked against them, for even those who had kept their jewels for the good King could not now enter till the Prince of Peace should bear their punishment, and, returning victorious over the robbers, should again open the golden gates.

"But the good King provided rest and safety for the aged and toil-worn people, and when those that had kept their jewels had fulfilled their years of labour, the white guards led them to a strong palace near the gates, where they were secure from the robbers, and could rest in peace until the Prince should come to crown them with victory.

"And so the years passed on, and the struggling people cried to the Prince to come and set them free, and the waiting people cried from their beds in the palace to him to hasten his coming, and he also wanted to come and fulfil his noble work, but he had not found a maiden with a clean heart that he could take for his mother.

"The white guards searched everywhere. They

went to the grand dwellings, and saw many a lovely lady who strove to keep her jewel for the King, but one had got a little pride, and another a little deceit, and another was hasty in her temper, and another, though she loved the King, loved herself at the same time. And day by day the white guards went home sorrowing, and said, ' No clean-hearted maiden can be found to be mother to the Prince of Peace.'

" At last they went to a little cottage home where an old man and woman were toiling hard from morning till night, and living scantily on the poorest food. Their young daughter too, was there, clad in coarse clothing, and spinning diligently. There were white guards there already, and when they saw the shining Ambassador they greeted him reverently, and pointed to the three hard-working people, and to each jewel pointed steadily to the King's throne. Those in the aged hearts had been manfully defended in many an assault of the robbers, but the girl's heart was pure as crystal, the blackness which had stained all other hearts since that first theft in the garden, was absent from hers, and the Robber could not find an entrance by which to attack her jewel.

" The peasants did not see the white guards, for they always made themselves invisible, and so they acted just as if they were by themselves altogether. The aged Ann turned to her daughter, and said, 'go to the well, child, and fetch water to clean the house.'

"The young Mary rose up instantly from her work; she had wished to spin just another handful of wool, but she loved still better to obey every word of her mother, because such deeds made her jewel brighter and brighter for the King. So she took the jug and hurried off to the cave where the spring was, with her heart full of love to the good King. And the shining messenger went on before her.

"Mary dipped her jug in the well and drew it forth full of clear water. She was lifting it to her shoulder, when the messenger appeared before her, and said, looking at the heart full of love:

"'Hail Mary, full of grace, the Lord is with thee!'

"Mary was astonished, and she trembled, and wished her mother was beside her, but the bright messenger comforted her.

"'Fear not, Mary,' he said, 'for I bring you good news. The good King has chosen you to be the mother of his Son, the Prince of Peace.'

"Still Mary could hardly understand, for she knew the greatness of the King, and she felt that she was nothing. She could not understand, but she felt at once that she was ready to do anything that the King might ask of her. So she made answer to the bright messenger :

" ' Behold the handmaid of my Lord, let Him do with me as He will.'

" Then the messenger went back to the King, and all the white guards came together and thanked him for having at last made so pure a maiden that the Prince could be her child, and they went to the Waiting Palace and told all the people resting there, that the mother was found who should have the child to bring them deliverance, and they also sang hymns of joy.

" So this, dear children, is the first mystery of your Rosary, and it is called the Annunciation. The maiden at the spring was the Blessed Virgin, and the bright messenger was the Angel Gabriel. All the people on earth, and those that were dead too, were waiting in hope till a pure virgin should be found to be the Mother of Jesus. When St. Gabriel saw her heart full of love, and without any sin in it, he cried with joy, ' Hail, full of grace,' just as we say on a birthday, ' I wish you happiness, I wish you a happy feast.' Among the many virtues in that maiden's heart, humility was the most attractive : she did not know that she was

pure and sinless, she did not think of herself at all.
We owe her much love for being so humble, and
we say the first decade of our Rosary to remind us
of the scene in the cave, when in obedience to her
mother, she went for water, and was too humble to
know how full her heart was of grace. Let us
kneel now and say these ten Hail Marys in her
honour, fancying that we see her with her water-
jug, and the bright angel at her side : and as we
congratulate her on the great favour shown her,
and wish her happiness and joy for all eternity, let
us pray to God to make us humble like her, and
like her, full of grace."

The children said the first Our Father, and ten
Hail Marys with great devotion, and then little
Christine crept close to her aunt.

"The Nunzishun is my picture, auntie, and I
think I have got humble now."

"You humble, Christine!" exclaimed Harry,
"why, you were looking at your new frock all the
time of Mass on Sunday."

Christine blushed deeply. "Yes, Harry, I know,
and mamma talked to me about it, and I am never
going to do so any more. Besides that is some
days ago, and I had not heard the story of the
Nunzishun."

"The An-nun-ci-a-tion, Christine," said Auntie.

" When a person tells a piece of news, it is called
an announcement. When the French and Prussian
war came to an end peace was *announced*, so in the
same way the Angel Gabriel *announced* the good
news that Mary was to be the Mother of Jesus,
and the scene is called the Annunciation."

" Yes, Auntie, and now that I have the picture
of the Annunciation, and know the story, it will
be sure to cure my pride. It is not easy not to
like my new frock, but I will try. Katy can better learn to be humble, for she scarcely ever has a
new frock."

Katy looked more sorry than glad at this, but
Jack said, " Please, ma'am, isn't there other ways
of being proud or humble than along of one's
clothes ?"

" There are many ways, Jack. When a boy in
a tidy jacket is ashamed of being seen with a poor
collier ;" here Eleanor gave an admonitory nudge to
her brother Tom, who blushed crimson; " or a
child is elated by getting up a step or two in the
Catechism class ;" both Jack and Katy had to blush
now ; " or a child is offended because at the school
cleaning she is set to wash the floor, while another
has to dust the pictures ;" it was Minnie's turn to
look abashed now; " or a girl tries to buy finery
with her earnings when others of the family have

need of the money ;" all eyes now turned on Polly, who wore a large sash round her waist ; " or a boy refuses to come to school one Sunday, because he was turned out for levity the week before ;" Johnny's bright eyes were downcast now ; " and in a hundred other ways the Robber tries to steal from us the jewel of humility. But remember, children, he cannot rob us against our will ; if we snatch at the humility when it is just going, we shall save it, and if it is quite gone, we can have it back by confessing our pride, and asking help from the Prince of Peace."

At this moment the Doctor put his head into the room. " Have you got my small Will of the Wisp there, Margaret ?" he asked.

Christine laughed for joy, but her spirits were quelled by the humbling truths she had been hearing of, so she nestled lovingly to her father, without any noisy merriment.

" I will carry her home," he said, " for it is raining cats and dogs. Here, Harry, wrap yourself in my great coat. Morris and Rivers are waiting in the school for their children. Mind you all get your mothers to put you to bed whenever you get home, little ones, for you will all be drenched to the skin."

Jack was busy taking off his jacket to put round

Katy, then he made her get upon his back, and thus they started across the swollen brook. Aunt Margaret saw them all off, and noticed the mischievous fun of little Johnny, when Polly had to lift up her sweeping skirt and show the ragged boots and stockings hitherto concealed. It was trying weather, but the children enjoyed the adventure of the wetting, and in another hour were all sleeping quietly in their beds.

STORY OF THE SECOND BEAD.

BROTHERLY LOVE.

AFTER some days, when the weather had become bright and clear, the children crossed the brook and the school-field by the light of the hunter's moon, and assembled once more round the table in the class-room on which the large Rosary lay. Aunt Margaret was getting some books out of the school library for some children who did not belong to her circle, so those around the table had time for a few words together before the story should begin. As usual, Christine was first to speak.

"I didn't ever once look at my new frock in church on Sunday," she whispered to Katy; "and when we had a tea-party I didn't ask to have my blue sash. Have you done anything, Katy, in memory of the Annunciation, and to please the humble Virgin?"

Katy glanced timidly round, and seeing that the boys were listening, she looked rather cross, and said, " I don't know."

" Yes she have, miss," cried Jack eagerly. " Mother had an old frock given her for Sundays, and she let her wear it, and Nora next door said as it was only beggars, and such low folks, as would wear cast clothes, and Katy was going to let her tongue loose on her, but I minded her of the humble Virgin at the well, and she ran into the house, and her and me said the beads about the Annunciation together. Didn't us, Katy ?"

" Yes," replied Katy ; then added with sparkling eyes, " but Nora told a lie about the cast clothes, for she has one on as a neighbour gived her this very day."

There was a little sound that was like a softly spoken " Hush !" and the Rosary on the table moved, though Christine was sure she had not shaken the table, but they all said that the second bead was raised above the others, and they listened attentively to what it might say. The voice then spoke.

" The second Mystery of the Rosary is what we have to learn about to-day. But who knows what a mystery is ?"

" The Annunciation is a mystery," replied Harry.

" True," said the voice, " but that does not ex-

plain the word.   A mystery is a truth that we can
partly understand, but which contains some more
truth that is impossible for men to understand in
this life.   The growth of a plant is a mystery, we
can easily see and understand the dropping of the
seed into the ground, and we can see the leaf
spring up, and the plant grow week by week, but
how the seed makes root and pushes up its blade,
and how the leaves grow one after another, is
what we know takes place, but can only partly
understand.   Again, we know when a hen sets on
eggs presently chickens come out of the eggs, and
grow and grow till they get to be cocks and hens.
The coming out of the chicks is easy to see and
understand, but how their limbs grow out of the
substance of the egg, and how the down comes
on their small bodies, and how that changes to fea-
thers after, is very difficult to understand.   These
are mysteries of the world about us.   Now we know
that the Mysteries of the Rosary are true, and we
can understand something about them, but they
contain many things that we can only fully understand when we have prayed and loved God all our
life long, and got at last into His good land, the
bright Heaven, where we shall know everything.

" Thus in the Mystery of the Annunciation every
one can easily imagine Mary at the well, and the
angel speaking to her, but the wonderful design of

God to make her the Mother of his Son, the need of Jesus coming and taking our nature upon Him, and of the purity of his Mother, we can only understand by little and little, and shall never come to see all the goodness and wisdom of God in it, till we get to him in Heaven.

"The second story is still about the humble and lowly Mary. When she heard that the King had chosen her for the office which all the fine ladies in the country had been longing for, she did not triumph or boast, she only thanked God, and ran to tell her parents the joyful news.

"In the good land there was a high mountain, on which the good King's palace was built, and from the windows of that palace he could see all over the new country. His sight was stronger than that of other people, for he could see through the walls of the houses, and under the trees, nay, more, he could see the jewel burning in every heart, and whether its flame turned towards him, or downwards towards the Robber's dark land.

"Thus he saw Mary at the well, and her sweet joy, and her absolute humility, and that her jewel's flame burned steadily upwards in faithful love to him.

"When Mary had told her parents, and they had all thanked the King with one glad voice, she began to long to tell her dear cousin Elizabeth.

Mary loved her cousin very much, though she was a grave old woman, while Mary was yet a very young girl, only fifteen."

"Only as old as you, Polly," said Jack, "and a bit younger than me and master Harry, for us be near sixteen !"

Polly smiled, and it was only then that Aunt Margaret noticed the absence of her brother.

"Where is your Johnny?" she asked.

"Please ma'am, he be working nights this week, he and Tim White; Jack there, and another lad will have to work nights next week, and then Johnny and Tim will come here."

"The story," whispered Christine, fidgeting on her chair.

All fixed their eyes again on the second large bead in the Rosary, and the voice proceeded.

"The young Mary asked leave of her parents to go across the mountains to see her cousin, and tell her the good news; and her parents were willing that she should do so, for Elizabeth was a wise and pious woman."

"It was a great feast at Jerusalem, and all the people were assembled to fulfil their duty, and the High Priest was conducting the service; it was something like the Mass, but the sanctuary was hidden from the people by a thick curtain.

" Well, the Priest was there alone with the Presence of God in the sanctuary, and a message from the good King came to him, that he would send him a little son. But Zachary thought the news was too good to be true, and he said,—' No, surely, after we have passed all these years childless, it is not to be expected that we should have a son now in our old age.'

" The King was displeased at Zachary for holding to his own opinions, instead of just believing the message he sent to him, so he punished him by striking him dumb, and he said he should remain dumb until the little son arrived, who would prove that the King's promise was a true one.

" When the Priest came out of the sanctuary he could not speak, for his tongue was fast tied, and he had to go home with Elizabeth in sadness and sorrow ; but he already repented of having doubted the King's word, and the King forgave him, and restored his jewel to its brightness, though he kept him dumb for the time appointed, as a fitting penance for his unbelief.

" It was while Zachary and Elizabeth were living quietly in their home, waiting for the gift of the King and the end of the penance, that the gentle Mary arrived at their house. She was very tired, for she had crossed the mountains on foot."

"Was she too poor to pay the railway fare?" asked Christine, sympathetically. "I would have given her some of my pennies if I had known."

"Maybe there wasn't no train; it's awkward making railways over mountains, us can't go by train to Machen," added Jack.

"Railways were not invented so long ago," resumed the voice, "and Mary had travelled on foot only. When Elizabeth saw her coming a new light came into her mind, and she knew the joy that had come to Mary before her cousin spoke. Mary saluted her kindly, and then Elizabeth replied, 'Blessed art thou among women, and blessed is the fruit of thy womb. Whence comes this honour to me, that the Mother of my Lord should come to me. And blessed art thou that hast believed, for the King will do all that he has promised!'

"You see Elizabeth had experienced the evil of disbelieving, for her poor husband was still suffering his penance of dumbness, whereas Mary, who had believed the message at once, was full of grace and joy.

"And Mary sat with her dear cousin, and poured

forth her joy and gladness. And she praised the good King for choosing her to bring up his sweet son, the Prince of Peace, telling Elizabeth how poor and unworthy she was, and that she had no claim to the King's favour except his own great goodness and love.

"They staid together a long time, for Elizabeth had also her tale to tell, how that one of the white guards had appeared by the side of the altar when her husband was offering the incense, and had promised him a son who should preach and teach the people to do penance, and prepare the way for the Lord. So the two cousins staid together, loving and helping one another, and counselling each the other how best to prepare for the children that were coming, and to serve and love the good King.

"This, then, is the story of the Blessed Virgin's Visitation, that is her visit to her cousin, and it shows how loving her heart was to those related to her. When we think of her fatiguing journey, and the sisterly love which made her travel so far to share her joy with her good cousin, we love her more, and say along with Elizabeth, 'Blessed art thou among women, and blessed is the fruit of thy womb. And blessed art thou which hast believed, for God is sure to make his promise good.'

"Besides thinking with pleasure of the loving conduct of the sweet Virgin, we must take care to imitate it. While we say the decade, or ten Hail Marys, in honour of her love to her cousin, we must beg of God to put such love into our own hearts also, that we may be willing to bear fatigue or loss for our brothers and sisters, our parents and friends, or for any who belongs to the family of God. Look at Jack's picture, there is the young and humble Virgin and her aged cousin conversing together of the love of God. Let us say the decade in their honour, seeking to be filled with just their loving spirit."

The children repeated the "Our Father" and ten "Hail Marys" devoutly. They had not finished the "Glory" when the door burst open, and little Johnny entered in haste, his teeth chattering, and his hands trembling.

"Oh madam, do come—come quickly. Tim's a near killed, and the lads is a carrying of him home. His mother's just out of her mind, and I'm a running for the doctor. Jack, lad, come along with me, I'm feared to go by myself."

There was short leave-taking. "Polly," said Aunt Margaret, "will you begin the work of brotherly love by taking Katy home? Harry, you can have charge of Christine. Go children, and

ere you rest to-night pray, as the loving Mary
would have prayed, for help for the afflicted
one."

Timothy's accident was not an uncommon one;
the earth had fallen in where the lads were working, and had broken his arm, while some sharp
stones had inflicted ugly cuts on his head, at sight
of which his mother had fainted away. When the
doctor came he set the arm and plastered up the
cuts. Aunt Margaret watched beside him to give
the medicine in case of feverish symptoms, for the
mother had never learned to control herself and so
was useless as a sick nurse.

For that night the work in the mine was suspended, as was the custom when any serious accident had occurred. Jack and his comrade went to
work in the morning, after a long consultation with
Johnny. Both that Saturday and the two following ones Christine and Harry brought their weekly
money to buy food or medicine for Timothy, and
after a hard struggle even the vain little Polly
sacrificed the few pence that she would have spent
on a fine ribbon, to help the sick lad.

Aunt Margaret suspended her evening classes,
for she gave so much time to the invalid, that she
had little left at her disposal, and both Jack and
Johnny assured her they could not attend, though

they would not tell her the reason. After three weeks, Timothy was able to walk about with his arm in a sling, and he thus made his appearance for the first time in the class room. Aunt Margaret welcomed him, and gave him an arm chair beside the fire, and told Harry to chat with him till others should arrive. It was not a Rosary evening, only one for learning Christmas hymns.

"Time must hang heavy during this illness," said Harry, "for I fear you cannot read."

"Read! I never had a chance of learning, and now there is no time, what with work, and what with hunger!"

"Are you so poor? Ah yes, I suppose you get no wages now?"

"Yes, I do," he said eagerly. "Them two lads has been working double tides, awearing themselves out to get the wages for me. But you see, sir, though they are so good, things is hard with me. There is a lot of us, and father is an old man, and he and mother, and all of us have neglected our religion, and when the wages are got they are gone directly, and we are starving half our time. The lads want me to come to Sunday school and night classes, and I'm willing, I'm sure; but in the starvation times I know I shall not have heart for anything!"

" Hope in God, Timothy. You are not in want now ?"

" No, sir, no. Folks has been good as angels. You, and little miss, and many another of the children, even Polly there, has brought me things ; and the lady has made me soup and nice drinks, and I have had clothes given, and a deal of good talk. I am all right now, and willing to try my best and learn my religion ; but I know my mind will alter when the bad times come."

" I say, Tim ; why should you not begin to learn to read ? I am so often ailing that I can't go to school. I will give you a lesson now and then."

" I haven't got no book, sir."

" I will find one that Christine has done with. And you shall sing too—you will get a lesson to-night. Christmas will be here directly, and it will be a nice change for you to go Christmas-singing. Is your mother better ?"

" She ain't no great things ; but Minnie is clearing up for her to-night, so the place will be tidy for once. Please, sir, to learn me a Christmas hymn, for the tune do come easier to me than the words."

By a little patience Timothy learned a hymn by heart, and the singing boys having arrived, he assisted at their practice. He has a nice voice and good ear, and he enjoyed his evening thoroughly, and went home greatly inspirited by a promise from the Priest that as soon as he could read he would take him into the choir, providing, of course, that his conduct was satisfactory.

STORY OF THE THIRD BEAD.

THE SPIRIT OF POVERTY.

HE glow of the pit fires had nearly died out, and all the labouring engines had rest, their heavy beating was stopped, and none of the blackened faces were to be seen around the mine's mouth, for the holiday of Christmas had begun, and for a couple of days there was rest alike for man and machinery.

The moon sailed solemnly through that Christmas sky, and looked down on the Welsh hills and their populated vallies, and for once she saw mankind asleep—collier and metal, smelter, forgeman, and stoker, all at rest.

But from out of many a house clean-washed faces began to appear long before the moon had run her course; along the lanes they came, and from the hill-sides, and a goodly number assembled in the newly-built chapel in the meadow by the brook.

They found the chapel gay with evergreens and
flowers and illuminations, all exclaiming either in
material letters, or in the spirit of their arrange-
ment there, "Glory to God in the Highest."

Little Christine came, holding tightly by her
father's hand, and joyful at the unwonted pleasure
of seeing the chapel so gaily lighted, and in the
general gladness of the feast. Jack and Johnny
had had to work late, for their visitation labour
was not yet finished; but they did not grudge the
early rising, but arrived in time to don cassock and
surplice, and assist in serving Mass.

Poor Timothy took his place for the first time in
the choir, his voice was a little tremulous, for his
heart was touched by his first lessons in the love
of God, but the prevailing joyfulness soon took
possession of his mind, and as the world wide song
began, his voice rose full and clear,

> "O come, all ye faithful,
>   Joyful and triumphant,
> To Bethlehem hasten with glad accord.
>   See in the manger,
>   The Monarch of angels,
> O come, let us adore Him, Christ the Lord."

There were some other worshippers there who had
never before rendered homage to the God of their
fathers. Willie and Teddy, the younger brothers

of Timothy, and sister Mary too, had ventured out under cover of the darkness to see what the new chapel was like, and to hear Tim sing. They were clothed in pitiful rags, and their inner raggedness was yet more pitiful, for they had never yet learned of Him who came to save their souls.

The hymns were sung, the prayers said, the great Sacrifice offered. Christine and Katy sat quietly afterwards, while those who had gone to Holy Communion made their thanksgiving; but when the Doctor moved, Christine glided before him to Katy's side, and grasped her hand instead of her father's; it ever seemed a necessity to Christine to be holding some hand.

"What!" said the Doctor, "are you going to forsake me, Chris?"

"Yes, papa, just this morning. You know we Rosary children are going to breakfast with Aunt Margaret in the class-room."

"Very well, my dear. Wait for your aunt, and don't go running about in the snow."

They had not long to wait. Minnie had darted away some minutes before, and had thrust lots of wood into the fire, so that when all the party arrived, the kettle was boiling loudly, and no one felt inclined to complain that there was a good deal of smoke in the room.

"Go to the fire, Jack; you look pale, and are trembling with cold," said Aunt Margaret, and Timothy glanced anxiously at his friend.

But when the hot tea was ready, and the Christmas cakes, the pale looks had disappeared, and all seemed equally glad of this first Christmas treat.

"What for did you tremble so?" asked Tom of Jack, in a low voice.

"What for! You'd have been shaking, lad, if you'd worked till nigh midnight, and then found you were too late for your supper. You do nothing but go to school, and then get your victuals and your rest, and you can't never be what I call tired!"

Tom looked cross, but Timothy interposed.

"Don't speak rough to him, Jack, he worked most as hard as a collier yesterday. Him, and Eleanor, and Ethel was a wanting to help me, they said they would do some visitation work, like the rest of you, only they didn't know how, and Mr. Rivers said, that if they would carry out all the parcels from his shop he would pay them nine-pence a piece. It wasn't a few parcels there was to carry, I can tell you; I carried what I could in my one arm, and I was tired, I know that."

This was said in a whisper, and all those that were busy eating missed hearing it. Jack gave

Tom's hand a hard gripe, and nodded to Eleanor and Ethel in token of fellow feeling, and then renewed attacks were made on the Christmas cake.

When the breakfast was finished, there was still an hour and a half to wait before High Mass, so the girls were set to remove the breakfast things, and then the big Rosary was placed on the table, and Aunt Margaret proposed the story of the Third Bead.

Every one looked glad when they saw the Rosary, for they had been a month without any fresh instructions about it.

"Timothy han't got no picter," said Jack, sorrowfully.

"Yes I have," the boy replied, "Master Harry have given me his. It is the lady with the little child, and the beasts around them."

"Why it's the very one for to-day !" cried Johnny, "the Blessed Virgin and the Infant Jesus in the stable. But you don't know the other Mysteries, Tim : you won't half understand the Third Bead's story."

"Master Harry have learned me about the Nun—"

"An-nun-ci-a-tion," interrupted Christine.

"About the Annunciation," continued Timothy,

"and every one of you has helped to learn me the Visitation, so I am as ready for the next as e'er a one of you."

Aunt Margaret gave the signal for attention, every eye turned on the large Rosary upon the table, and especially on the Third Bead, which now lay uppermost. This time the voice began with questions.

"If you children were princes and princesses, and had to begin life anew, would you be born rich or poor?"

"Rich!" cried all the children, in one voice.

"*Where* would you be born?"

"In a good warm house, where there was a rousing fire," said Jack.

"In a very pretty room, with pictures all round," said Chistine.

"In a good place where there was plenty of victuals and coals, and a good bed to lie on," said Timothy.

And all the others chose comfortable and handsome homes.

"And what kind of people would you be?" asked the voice.

"I would be a princess," said Christine, "and wear best frocks always, and have plenty of toys, and some one to learn my lessons for me."

"I would be the squire's son, and ride a pony of my own," said Tom.

"I would be like little miss at the Castle, and have blankets and coals to give away at Christmas," said Ethel.

"I would somehow have lots of money, so that father and mother shouldn't work, and I would make a lady of Katy there," said Jack.

"And I would be strong and well, and go to college, and skate and ride, and do everything that other boys do," said Harry.

"I would be a lady and get married," said Polly.

"Listen, children," resumed the voice. "When the Prince of Peace knew that the time was come for his great work, and that a sinless maiden was found to be his mother, he resolved to come down to the new country. He could have made Mary a queen at once, and brought all his white guards to wait upon her, but he did not do it. The thing he was coming to live and die for was this—to make the people of the new country love and serve the King his Father faithfully during their time of trial, and so to win back the sweet homes in the Good Land which had been got ready for them, but which they had lost all claim to by their disobedience. The Prince knew that it was only by humility, and love, and faith, and obedience, that the good King could be pleased, so he made it his one object to teach these virtues both by his word and his example. There was another person who knew the way back to the Good Land, only he could not follow it, and that was the Robber-king, so he spent all his strength in trying to teach people pride, and hatred, and unbelief, and disobedience."

"I won't have nothing to do with him, he's a real bad 'un," exclaimed Jack, and all the children shook their heads in sympathy.

"So the Prince who had the choice of everything chose to be very poor. The King had sent a message to a good carpenter, that he should marry Mary, in order to help her to take care of the Prince when he should be born, and a little while before his birth, the Roman emperor had ordered every person to go to his own parish in order to pay the taxes which he required of them. So Joseph and Mary went together across the country to Bethlehem.

"When they got there they found that the place was full of richer people, who could pay more for lodgings than they could, and as they could find no house to stay in, they were forced to put up with a stable. There it was that the Prince of Peace arrived; there was no bed to lay him on, only coarse straw, and no cradle for him, so Mary had to lay him in a manger. No one in the town noticed these people, nor cared for the new-born child any more than they do for the baby of an Irish beggar woman ; they danced, and sang, and quarrelled, and fought, and eat, and drank, and never looked toward the stable where the little Prince lay.

" The King sent no message to any of the rich people, he did not want them about his dear child, they were selfish and proud, and the Robber-king had stolen most of their jewels, and they never cared to try to get them back again.

" But the white guards sang in the King's Palace, and made the Good Land ring with their music, singing to golden harps, ' Glory to God in the Highest, and on earth peace to men of good will.'

" There were some poor shepherds keeping watch over their sheep all night. The fine folks in Bethlehem thought no more of them than they did of the infant in the manger, but the poor shepherds loved the good King, and the flame of their jewels burned steadily upwards towards his throne. They were cold and poor now, but they hoped some day to have good homes in the Good Land. Suddenly as they watched, fearing lest some wild beast should come to devour their sheep, one of the white guards stood beside them, and his clothes shone all over like the King's crown, and the shepherds were sorely frightened. But the guard spoke, and said, 'Do not be afraid, I bring you glad and joyful news—the Prince is born, who will save all you people from the robbers. He is lying in a manger at Bethlehem,' and as he finished speaking, a multitude of the shining singers appeared in the sky, and they sang as they had already done about the King's throne, 'Glory to God in the Highest, peace on earth to men of good will.'

" When they had gone, and the poor shepherds had recovered from their surprise, they saw that the morning was beginning to dawn, so they were no more uneasy for their flocks, the wild beasts being afraid to molest them by day-light. They therefore agreed that they would go to Bethlehem, and see the Blessed Infant, and offer him the love of their hearts.

" A long, long way off, in quite a distant valley, three learned men were praying to the King, and watching the moon and stars, thinking that the King might send them messages by the different stars. And as they looked up into the sky, and admired the work of the Creator, they saw a star that they had never seen before. They were astonished, and they read in the books which their fathers had left them, and saw that about that time the Prince was to be born. And their hearts were glad, and they said the star must be a messenger from the King to guide them to the Saviour.

"So they went to their house, and took some presents. These men were rich, but they loved the King more than their riches, and were ready to leave them at once without any one to guard them, while they went to pay respect to the Saviour Prince. They took some of their gold, and sweet spices, and perfumes, as presents, with them, and to shew him that they were willing to give him everything they had.

"And Mary and Joseph watched over the little babe, and took care of him. Mary sang him sweet songs, and pressed him to her breast, and made her arms a cradle for him, as he had no other. Early in the morning the shepherds came, and they knelt and worshipped the little baby, and loved him, and praised him, and went back to their sheep.

"The three wise men had to travel many days, and cross the mountains on foot, and wade across the rivers ; but still the faithful star went on before them, and still they followed, looking at every fine house to see if the infant Prince was there. But the star went near none of these houses, so the wise men did not stop.

"At last they came near Bethlehem, and the star went on. When it did stop, it was over the door of a stable! The wise men trusted to the star, feeling sure that it was the King's own sign, and when they entered the stable, there lay the baby on his Mother's knee, wrapped in a coarse garment, like the children of the poor, and his Mother and Joseph as poorly clad as possible. But the wise men had wisdom enough to disregard outside appearances, and they knelt and did homage to the Prince, and offered him their gifts, their hearts, and their all.

"The sweet Prince chose to be poor to teach us that poverty is a help in our way to heaven. It is not that riches of themselves make us sin, only that we get to think of ourselves, and to indulge ourselves when we can have whatever we desire. This life here is only a preparation for a far, far longer life elsewhere. The poor long more for the good land of heaven than the rich do—the rich are sometimes so comfortable that they would be content here for ever, but the poor look constantly upwards, or ought to do so, for therefore was poverty sent. Poverty draws us nearer to God, and when we think of the Mystery of the Nativity, or birth of Jesus, we should pray for the Spirit of Poverty."

There was no answering smile on the faces of her little audience, as Aunt Margaret looked around, and Tim's eyes were full of tears. A long silence ensued, and the poor boy was the first to speak, his eyes were fixed on his picture, and his voice trembled. "Cold and hunger and quarrelling and misery come of poverty, ma'am. Us can't bring our minds to pray for these !"

"Assuredly not, my poor boy; but the good God does not wish these to come. He would have us look cheerfully up to Him for our daily bread, working diligently to earn it at the same time, and not being anxious for the morrow. But for sin, our own or other people's, honest labour would always be able to earn food, and fire, and clothing ; it is the Robber-king who allures to the beer-house, and so robs children of the necessaries of life. Riches would not prevent sorrow coming in by the way of the public-house."

"No ma'am, no. I wouldn't mind poverty if the children had food and clothing"—he could not say more, for a sob choked him.

"Please ma'am," said Ethel gently, "if riches are so hurtful, why did God make any rich ?"

"It is the will of God that people should win

heaven or hell by their own choice, dear child. To every one He gives this choice one way or another. The state of riches that is dangerous to the soul is the spending money and thought on one-self. One man might have a thousand pounds in his pocket, and another only ten pounds. The man with the thousand might spend on himself only just enough for health and decency, and spend the rest on objects of charity and piety, so as to please God and benefit his own soul by every one of the thousand pounds; while the man with ten pounds might so lay it out in eating and drinking and self-pleasing, as to make every shilling a cause of sin to himself and others, and a step towards the loss of his soul. I ought not to have said we should desire poverty, but the Spirit of Poverty, that is, the resolution to spend only what is really necessary on ourselves. Christine's wish for the princess's gay clothes, Tim's for the squire's pony, and Polly's for the luxuries of a lady, were all of the kind that make riches selfish and dangerous."

"But Jack's wish to have money that his mother shouldn't work, and Ethel's to have blankets for the poor, were they the right kind of way of wanting riches?" asked Eleanor.

"Such would have been the right way of spending the riches if God had sent them, my dear.

But all wishing is foolish, for God knows so much better what is good for us than we do. Let us say the decade for the Nativity, praying to the Prince of Peace, who came and made himself one of us to-day, that He will give us the Spirit of Poverty, making us unselfish in all our actions, and comforting all who suffer from the evils of poverty which sin has caused."

There was many a moist eye as the prayers were said, for poor Timothy was still crying. When the Rosary was finished, the bell for the second Mass began to sound, and Christine and Harry ran off to meet their mamma. Jack and Johnny bustled off to get ready to serve again, and the other children hastened in different directions. Ethel only waited for the lady, and as Tim passed her, she said,—

"Please to call this afternoon to taste our cake, Timothy, and bring some of the little ones. Mother says you will be kindly welcome."

When the boy was gone, it was the lady's turn to question.

"What makes Timothy feel poverty so keenly, Ethel? Those other lads have done his work for him, so that his wages have come in regularly, and you have all helped him, for which may God bless you!"

"It is along of his mother, ma'am. She got her husband's wages on Saturday, and the few pence us Rosary children got together, and his wages too, and she went and bought flour and tea, and then stopped at the public. Mother called round there last night to take them a cake, and there wasn't a bit of cleaning done, nor a bite of bread in the house, and it will be the same to-day likely. Mother gave them the cake among them, for the mother hadn't come in; but Tim wouldn't taste it, he said it should be for the little ones. It's my belief he hadn't had food in his mouth from yesterday morning till your breakfast."

Poor Timothy didn't go home till after the High Mass. When he got there he found all just as Ethel had described it, the house was dirty, no fire in the grate, the mother cross and ill, and of course the children crying. Tim prayed to the great God, who chose poverty for his inheritance, to help him to bear its crushing evils.

"Come along Tim, lad," cried the rough voice of Jack; "mother says she wants you to learn our Katy that tune you can sing—come and sit beside our fire. Little Bill and Ted, come along!"

The three brothers made many a visit that Christmas day, for Bill and Ted could dance like real Irish boys, and the old exiles loved to see it, and between a slice of cake in one house, and a hunch of bread and cheese in another, the poor little urchins got their hunger satisfied, and even their pockets filled.

And Minnie and Eleanor put off their tidy frocks, and went and cleaned up Mrs. White's house; it was a great sacrifice to them, for they had earned their holiday by diligence, and they loved it well; and Mr. Rivers, who dealt in coals as well as provisions, sent a basket-full to the house, for he as well as the other neighbours agreed that though the woman was very faulty, cold and hunger were out of place among Christian people on a Christmas day.

STORY OF THE FOURTH BEAD.

OBEDIENCE.

"WHAT kind of story will the Fourth Bead tell?" asked Christine, whose tongue could not lie still, until her aunt took her place among the children. "The First told us about the Annunciation and Humility, the Second about the Visitation and the Love of our Neighbours, and the Third about the Nativity and the Spirit of Poverty. You see I don't forget anything, Harry."

"You remember the words and the stories very well, Chris, but you know there is something else more difficult to remember."

"You mean *doing* the things—yes, to be sure!" She blushed and remained silent a moment, but ever outspoken, even when speaking was hurtful to herself, she asked, "Do you really care for a doll, Katy?"

It was Katy's turn to blush. She was a shy child, and disliked having attention called to her, but, after struggling a moment for courage, she said, " I never had a doll ; mother has to spend all her money in victuals for us."

"Christine thinks you are too womanly to play with a doll," said Harry. "Is it so, Katy?"

"Mother do say she be too old-fashioned," put in Minnie.

"For shame to say so, Minnie," retorted Katy, with indignation. "I should like a doll very much, but I can't have one, so where's the good of talking !"

"If you will go home with me, after the story, I will give you a doll, Katy," said Christine, looking lovingly into her dark little face. "Mamma gave me a beautiful new one at the New Year, and Harry says it is not the Spirit of Poverty for me to have more than I can play with at a time. I like my old doll, and feel sorry to part with it, only I shall not be sorry to give it to you, dear Katy, it is so nice to please you."

Katy did not know what to say, but the very thought of the doll made her look ever so much less old-fashioned. Christine did not notice that her aunt had entered, and she quite started when she said, "There is some one else who is pleased

4

when we do an act of unselfishness who is dearer to us even than little Katy."

Christine's sweet face beamed with joy. "You mean the Infant Jesus, dear Aunty. Yes, it is nicest of all to please him who left his beautiful home on purpose to be poor for our sakes!"

None of the other children had spoken, but not one word had been lost on any of them, and many of the little hearts were questioning themselves as to their own special selfishness. All were glad when the voice sounded again, and the Fourth Bead lay uppermost.

"The good King had made all kinds of rules and regulations to remind the poor people of the new country to fight against disobedience, and all the other snares of the Robber, and to turn their hearts ever lovingly towards their promised homes in the Good Land. And among these rules was one requiring every firstborn son to be given to the King, and the mother at the same time to bathe her soul so as to wash it quite clean.

"Now Mary's soul had never been dirtied, she had never been disobedient, or proud, or selfish, or angry, she had always behaved submissively and affectionately to the King, to her parents, and to all her friends.

"But Mary knew that every act of obedience

was dear in the eyes of the good King, and shone like a fresh jewel on the brow as he looked down from his throne on the mountain. So, though her soul was not dirty, she went to wash it, and, though her child was the King's own Son, she took him to the Palace gate to present to her Lord.

"The King and all his thousands of white guards had seen all along the sweet jewels of humility and poverty glittering on Mary's brow, but now another sparkling jewel was added, the gem of Obedience.

"When she got to the Palace gate there were two old and tried servants of the King waiting with loving hearts until the messenger should come to take them to the Waiting Palace, where the cruel Robber could not come. As soon as they saw the sweet infant in Mary's arms, they knew that he was the Prince of Peace, though his clothes were such as the poor wear, and the man took him in his arms, and praised the King, and asked him now to take him away from the dangerous country, for that the Saviour was come, and there would be short detention in the Waiting Palace.

"And the King sent to tell Mary that she and Joseph should bring up the Prince for him, and so they took them to their poor cottage at Nazareth, where Joseph worked as a carpenter.

"Now, dear children, you have been told of the value of obedience until you are tired of the word, but, when you see the sinless Mary practising it, and Jesus the Son of God obeying her every word, and that of Joseph, too, you must see that we are not asking too much of you. Do you remember what the Priest said yesterday morning about obedience?"

"Yes" and "Yes" and "Yes" sounded on all sides, and then Jack said, "He told us he would teach us every Sunday afternoon, and he ordered us by the authority God had given him that we should attend. He said we should get a great blessing by obedience, and a heavy curse by disobedience."

"Very true; but who will send that curse—that punishment, I would rather say?"

"God," answered all solemnly — and Johnny exclaimed as if involuntarily, "And it has come," and he began to cry.

"How, Johnny? What do you mean?" asked Aunt Margaret.

"My little cousin, ma'am, poor little Nelly—she was such a good little 'un. She did beg to come to school, and they wouldn't let her, and now she will never come—never." The child was sobbing violently.

"Why won't she come, Johnny; she isn't dead!" asked Christine.

"May be not, miss; but she must die. It was last night it happened, just when we were all at Catechism with his Reverence. Uncle and aunt went out for a bit of rest, and to see folks, and Nelly was left to mind the young 'uns; the kettle boiled over, and she tried to take hold of it with her pinny, and the fire caught it, and Nelly ran out crying murders, and all in flames. She's burnt so that you wouldn't know her, but it was no fault of hers!"

"Was it her parents' fault then?" asked Jack.

"To be sure it was. Aunt and uncle knows it now, and would give their lives to have done different; but that won't save Nelly's life."

"Do people go to hell for disobedience, aunt?" asked Christine.

"Yes, Christine, they go by thousands; it is the old story that began six thousand years ago. Adam and Eve lost Paradise by disobedience—it was not the value of the apple, but the test whether they would obey God or themselves. The difference between sin and virtue is the same in all ages; to disobey a plain command of God given in his word or by the Church, be it in ever so small a thing, is sin; to obey in great things, or in little, is virtue.

The one displeases God, the other causes Him joy.

"Obedience is the lesson of the Fourth Mystery, the Presentation of our Infant Lord. All these Mysteries are joyful ones, so we must not grieve and sorrow about them. It is true that we cannot help grieving at the sight of pride and hatred and selfishness and disobedience, but there is a smiling side even to these dark pictures. The Prince of Peace came to procure pardon for sin, and to make us a present of his own graces. When our hearts convict us of an act of pride, or selfishness, or disobedience, we must be very sorry to think that we have done what will vex our loving Lord, and please the cruel Robber, but we are not to go on grieving. When we are sorry and confess our sin, we receive full pardon; and not only that but Jesus gives us of His own beautiful humility and unselfishness and obedience, so that after our sorrowful confession we are adorned with the jewels on our brow, which our Lord won for us. To-day we cannot but weep for the suffering of dear little Nelly, but the thought of the perfect obedience of Jesus consoles us. We will pray to Him to save the child from suffering, and to give her parents a full pardon."

"Oh, aunty, do let us go to Nelly and say the

obedience prayers with her," exclaimed Christine; and all answered in chorus, "Oh do let us go, do let us go."

Nelly's house was a long way off, but the day was fine, and the distance was not too great; so Aunt Margaret granted the childrens' urgent request. She entered the cottage alone first, to ascertain if the presence of the children would be suitable.

The suffering child lay on a low bed in the corner, and her father sat by her, his blackened face showing that he had recently come from the coal-pit. He was weeping bitterly, and the little sufferer was trying to comfort him, but in vain.

The child was fearfully burnt, especially about the face and neck; she had suffered very much when the dressings were put on, and for some hours afterwards, but now she felt easier—her little brother and sister sat on the hearth-stone, looking scared, and the weeping mother rocked the baby in her arms. No attempt had been made at cleaning the house, or washing the children, and all looked as wretched as it was possible to look.

"Nelly, darling," said the lady, "would you like the Rosary children to come in and say their beads beside you; they are so sorry for your misfortune, and they have begged me to bring them to see you once more."

"I should like them to come very much—I know the 'Our Father'. and 'Hail Mary' to say with them. I don't know any more prayers."

Heavy sobs burst from the poor father. "Oh," he cried, "may God have mercy on us! If only we had sent our little lass to the Priest, and she was wanting to go, she wouldn't have been taken from us. Let the bairns in, madam, the more prayers we can get the better, for our hearts are just broken!"

The children came and knelt round the bed; they had promised not to speak, except in the prayers, or to make any noise, and they tried hard to be very quiet and composed. Aunt Margaret began the Rosary, and all the young voices joined with deeply earnest devotion.

Little Nelly's voice spoke with the others. She knew nothing of the different Mysteries, but she knew that there was a loving Father in Heaven who was calling her to Him, and that a loving Saviour had come down on earth to open the way upward to Heaven. She knew that "Holy Mary, Mother of God" was one of the inhabitants of heaven, most frequently called upon by the poor sufferers on earth. She made her responses with a loving and trusting heart, and at every prayer, her pain grew less, and the home of perfect rest drew nearer to her.

Just as the Rosary was finished, the Priest arrived to anoint the little pilgrim for her short journey. Connolly's sobs burst forth anew, but Nelly smiled and said: "Oh, Father, let me go, for I see the Saviour holding out his arms for me."

Aunt Margaret called the children from the cottage, and Connolly followed them to the door. Once outside the little hearts felt free, and Christine hid her face in her aunt's dress, and burst into tears. Katy, and the twin Rivers sobbed likewise; indeed, every child was weeping.

" God bless the little 'uns," said Connolly, as he drew his hand across his eyes; " they haven't much to cry for, it's me and the mother that has got broken hearts for not sending the bairns when the Priest told us. It's hard work, madam, here at the mouth of the mine, to manage things anyhow, for it's such a long way for little children to go to school, and the lads at the tin works down there are awfully mischievous, and molest the bairns shockingly in passing. But if they molest them ever so the others shall go on Sundays. Oh, my little Nelly! my little Nelly! I wish I could have died for thee, only my soul isn't fit to go before God !"

"You can make it fit, my friend," said the lady. "When your little darling is safe with God, you will make a good confession, and then begin a new life. You know our Blessed Lord made Himself one of us to procure pardon for all our sins, and help for all our weaknesses. You and your children must now try to be the best Catholics in the place. God loves you now that you are in sorrow, as a mother or a father loves a suffering child, and he will no more be hard on you than you could be hard on your own Nelly. Go now and help to pray for her dear soul, and God will bless yours in doing it."

"Oh, Aunty!" cried Christine still sobbing, when her aunt joined her. "I would give my new doll and my best frock, and my blue sash too, if it could save the life of little Nelly. Do let us hasten home, and get papa to go to her, perhaps he could do something to cure her wounds."

"He has done all he could, darling. It is painful to part with her, especially for her parents, but it will be a great gain to Nellie. Jesus has washed her soul in His blood, and made a place ready for her in heaven. The lowly Virgin Mary will receive her there, and the holy angels be around her. Nelly will be brighter and happier than you have ever been, even on your birthday, when you tried to be ' quite good.' "

"And must she go ?" asked Christine, becoming more composed, "can we not keep her by praying ?"

"You would not keep her in that miserable place, all in the dirt, and her body covered with wounds, when she could go and be happy with Jesus in heaven, would you, Christine ?" asked Harry, in return, the light in his eyes told plainly enough what his own desires were.

Christine sighed; she was too sincere to say "no" when she felt "yes," but she saw she was wrong, so added, "I know it would be against the Visitation to say 'yes,' Harry, for it would be unkind to her. But here is papa, let us ask him."

The Doctor overtook them on horseback just as they reached the village. He answered Christine's question solemnly.

"God's will is ever best, my little daughter, for He loves us better than father, or mother, or little companions can do, and He always knows what will make us most happy in the long-run. He has proved His love for little Nelly by taking her to Himself : she only lived ten minutes after you had left, just long enough to receive Extreme Unction. Here we are at home, say good-bye to your companions, and come and tell mamma all about it."

Christine was crying, but she suddenly exclaimed,

" Oh, stop, Katy, till I bring you the doll; .I must not forget to do the Poverty."

Her father smiled, and Katy was delighted with her present, and hurried home to tell her parents the mingled tale of joy and sorrow.

STORY OF THE FIFTH BEAD.

ZEAL FOR GOD'S SERVICE.

"WHO got the Presentation picture?" was eagerly asked, when the children assembled again, for in the excitement of the visit to poor Nelly the picture had been forgotten.

Johnny laughed and blushed. "It was me as got it, just because it don't fit me at all," he said. "Mother do say that I be awfully bad at doing as I am bid."

"Well, I got Poverty, which I didn't like till the lady explained what part of it God sent, and what the devil made," rejoined Timothy. "Somehow I seem to have found it better to bear since, and now that I am at work again, and more out of the muddle, I get very fond of my picture."

"Isn't that queer?" said Christine, "I got the Annunciation, and I have got the least humility, but I have been better since, haven't I, Harry?"

"Ever so much better, dear; and Johnny has been more obedient, I suspect. Shall I call and ask your mother, Johnny?"

"No, no," said Johnny, eagerly; "no tales out of school, it isn't fair."

"No, it isn't, Johnny, and I will neither tell any, nor ask any questions. In our Rosary circle we must be able to speak our minds freely. You shall tell us yourself about your obedience, or we will be content to remain in ignorance."

"That will be about it," said Johnny, with a knowing skake of the head, "let us hear what Tom has to say about his picture, that is the one for to-day."

"I must first hear the Bead's story, for I can't read the picture myself. Here is a child standing be rt a lot of old men, there is glory about his head, so I fancy it is our Blessed Lord."

"Hush, Johnny, hush; see the Fifth Bead is uppermost, it is going to speak," cried Katy.

"After the holy Mother had offered her baby Son at the palace gate, and then taken him home again, a great danger arose. One of the Robber's people got hold of the three wise men, and questioned them about the baby in the manger, and when he learned from them that he was the Prince of Peace, he set his heart on killing him. So he gave orders that all the children under two years old should be killed, and he thought that he should get this done before the good King could hear ought about it. But the good King knew before even the words were spoken, because from his mountain he could look right into people's hearts, and one of the white guards was sent as quickly as the lightning flash to tell Joseph and Mary to go away into Egypt as quickly as ever they could. So when the cruel people came to kill the children, the Prince of Peace was gone away to a distant part of the country.

"When all was safe again, the white guard came again to Joseph, and told him to take his wife and the Prince back to their own country, and so they went and lived quietly at Nazareth. Joseph worked at his trade as a carpenter, and with his wages Mary bought food for them all. The royal child behaved just as if he was the carpenter's own son, obeying his young Mother and Joseph, doing such light work as they bade him do, and content to eat the same poor food that they eat. Year by year there was nothing to distinguish him from other children, only he was always humble, and kind, and obedient, and anxious to do everything to please his father.

"Another of the rules that the King had made

required that every one in the new country should go once a year to a certain city to swear fidelity to him, and to do him homage. Every child even had to go as soon as they were twelve years old.

"So when the Prince of Peace got to that age, his Mother and Joseph took him up to Jerusalem to the Feast. There he came to the great temple of the King, and saw the servants of the King, who were most learned about the laws and wishes of their Master. The young Prince was always thinking how best to win men to love his Father, that they might both love and obey, and so be made fit for the beautiful homes that stood ready for them in the Good Land.

"When the Feast was over, Mary and Joseph set off home again. A great number of people had gone along with them from Nazareth, for there were both wild beasts and robbers in the country they had to pass along, and they were glad of a good company that might defend one another. The Prince was not beside Mary when they started, but she thought she saw him with some other boys that belonged to the company, and she knew he could do no wrong, so left him to walk with whom he pleased.

"But when they had got a long way from Jeru-

salem, she called her son to her, and he was no-
where to be found. She was in great trouble, and
so was Joseph, and after asking every one in the
company, and finding that no one knew anything
about him, she became more alarmed still, and she
and Joseph resolved to go back to Jerusalem to
seek him. They forgot all they had heard about
wild beasts and robbers, and thought of nothing
but the loss of their beloved child.

"When they reached Jerusalem, footsore and
weary, they hurried to the temple, and there they
found their lost child, sitting quietly among the
learned men, asking them questions, and listening
humbly to their answers. He was all eagerness to
learn about the desires and wishes of the King.

"They were glad at heart to find him, you may
be sure, but Mary said to him in gentle reproach,
'Son, why have you done this? We have been in
great trouble about you, and have sought you in
sorrow,' and the child replied as gently, 'But why
did you seek me? Didn't you know that I should
be about my Father's business?'

"Thus you see that the Prince, even at twelve
years old, was eager to serve his King and Father,
first by learning how best to please him, and then
by practising all that he had learnt.

"I do not need to tell you, dear children, that

5

this Prince of Peace is our own blessed Lord Jesus,
who came down on earth, not only to· die for our
sins, and teach us how to die happily, but also by
his own life to shew us how to live. He was born
in poverty to teach his people to be content with
little, and to use such possessions as they might
have unselfishly. He was presented to God in the
temple to teach us holy and loving obedience to
God, and those God has placed over us, parents,
priests, teachers. He staid listening to the learned
men in the temple, to teach children to desire instruction, and to be patient and diligent in school,
and all of us to be anxious and zealous in the service of God. Tell me, children, how can we do
our heavenly Father's business, have we ever been
zealous in serving God ?"

No one spoke, and the lady saw she must put
personal questions to ensure the children under-
standing what she would explain, so she began with
the youngest—

"Christine, have you ever done anything to serve
God ?"

"I don't know," was the answer, for the child
was puzzled.

"Katy, have you ?"

"No, ma'am," was the reply.

"Johnny ?"

" Ne'er a hand's turn, ma'am ; and I don't know how to do it."

" Nor you, Jack ?"

" Nor me, neither, ma'am."

" Dear, dear, Minnie, you have surely done something ?"

" Yes, ma'am, I've learned some of my Catechism."

" Good. I am sorry none of the others have attended instructions."

" Oh, if that's it, so have I," said Johnny, his eyes sparkling, and his manner all alert again.

" And I," " and I," " and I," said the rest.

" Who got me the evergreens to dress the chapel for Christmas ?" asked the Lady.

" Jack and me, and Tim there fetched a couple, but we were over busy to do much," said Johnny.

" We will do a deal more for you next year," said Timothy gratefully.

" I believe the girls got the most this year, but most of you had a smaller or larger share in the work. Whose house were we dressing ?"

" God's house, ma'am.",

" Well, I declare !" exclaimed Johnny, " us have all been doing Christ-in-the-Temple work without knowing it !"

"Most true, Johnny. And what is it you do every Sunday, you and Jack?"

"What, serve at the altar, ma'am?"

"Yes, but who is it that comes on to the altar in Holy Mass?"

"Jesus Christ, ma'am."

"Then whom are you serving?"

"Why, to be sure, our Blessed Lord."

"And whom do you praise in singing your hymns, Timothy?"

The boy looked perplexed, for he had been so long neglected, that he was very slow.

"To whom do you sing glory?"

"Glory to God in the Highest," answered Timothy.

"To whom?"

"To God."

"Good. Then you sing to please God; you therefore are doing Christ-in-the-Temple work. Now tell me if you can think of any other ways of 'doing our Father's business?'"

"I have thought of one way, aunt."

"Tell it to us, Harry."

"Papa likes me to take exercise every day, and I may as well walk towards the mine as in any other direction. I will fetch Connolly's children to school every morning, and they can bring their dinners with them ; this will ensure their getting instruction."

" And I will do my best to make our little 'uns go to school, that will be a turn at Temple work for me," said Timothy.

" I've got no one to bring," said Christine, sadly ; " and there will be no more decorations to put up till Easter."

" Then you must honour Christ in the Temple by your own attention at school and in chapel, and by trying to remember all that you learn there."

" Yes, aunty."

" Please, ma'am, is it Christ-in-the-Temple work to sweep the school ?" asked Ethel, gently.

" Certainly it is, Ethel."

" Then I shall not dislike doing it any more."

" I also have disliked it, but I will do it willingly now," said Eleanor.

" And I will get the schoolmistress a bundle of sticks now and again," said Jack.

" I'll do it turn about," said Johnny ; " but what will you do, Polly ?"

" I have to slave all day at the works ; I can't get sticks, nor fetch children to school, nor do anything but come to Rosary myself, can I, ma'am ?"

" There is one thing, I think, you could do on Sundays, Polly ; but I don't like finding Temple work, as you call it, for you; I had rather you picked it out for yourself."

"But I don't know what it is, ma'am."

"It would suit either you or Eleanor. Which ever of you find it out first can have it, or you can take it as Johnny says, 'turn about.'"

"Is it to bring anyone to school?"

"No, not to school, she is too old for that?"

"To chapel?" exclaimed Eleanor.

"Yes, to chapel!"

"I know, I know," cried Tom, "It is blind Martha. Yes, ma'am, to be sure either Eleanor, or me, or Polly could bring her."

"Polly likes better to go with some wild girls who are choked up with all sorts of finery," said Johnny.

"Hush, Johnny; there must be no cross words in our Rosary; if we can't speak to help or please one another, we must keep silence."

"I will bring blind Martha, if Eleanor will take it turn about," added Polly.

"Agreed," said Eleanor.

"But isn't that visitation work?" asked Ethel.

"Works of love to God, and of love to our neighbour are very much alike, Ethel; indeed, they are generally mixed up together. When we labour for the good of our neighbour we act in the spirit of the Visitation, but we are generally working for God at the same time. Just in the same way when we work for God we also help our neighbour. The boys who serve at the altar, and sing in the choir, work for God ; but the congregation is also aided in their devotions, and so the neighbour also is served. When children are brought to instructions, and people to chapel, it is for the glory of God, but the soul of the neighbour gets benefit also. The same when the sick are tended, the ignorant taught, the hungry fed, the neighbour is served, but God also is pleased. We may well be greedy of the chances of both kinds of service, for we please God by both, and get bright jewels for our crown in heaven."

Katy glided off her chair, and went and whispered to Jack, and then Jack spoke.

"Please, ma'am, is there any way in which little 'uns like our Katy can do Temple work ?"

"There are doubtless many ways in which both she and Christine and the twin Rivers may do it after a little while. Both Katy and Christine have learned to hem nicely ; if they wish it, I will give them each a little napkin to hem that is needed for the altar. Girls cannot do rough work, such as fetching sticks and coals, and carrying heavy things, but sewing is a great resource to them ; I

will teach all the Rosary girls to work for the
altar if they will be patient in learning.   Then the
Society for the Propagation of the Faith is a grand
way of doing Temple work.   Those who can spare
a halfpenny a week can be enrolled as members of
it ; but those who can only give a halfpenny,
sometimes will be doing some Temple work.
This money goes to pay the cost of Priests going to the Pagans, to teach them about Jesus
Christ.   When I have time I can tell you stories
of the conversion of these pagans that are like fairy
stories for interest, but you must learn the Rosary
well first."

"Please, ma'am," said Ethel, "me and my little
sisters will bring a halfpenny a week, 'turn about,'
so that they shall have a hand in the Temple work."

"Now then, we are all satisfied," said Jack.
Master Harry will fetch the Connollys, Johnny
and me will get sticks, Timothy will send his
brothers, Polly and Eleanor will lead old Martha,
Tom will serve at the altar, Ethel and her sisters
will give halfpence.   Katy and Miss Christine will
hem napkins, and Minnie will sweep, turn about,
with the others."

"Yes, all are satisfied," said Aunt Margaret;
"now let us say the ' Our Father' and Ten ' Hail
Marys' in honour of the zeal of our Blessed Lord

in the Temple, and to beg of Him the grace to shew us how we may serve him, and to enable us to serve him well. We may well call these fine Joyful Mysteries, for they all make plain to us so many ways of pleasing God, and helping our own souls; and the same good Lord who shows us the way, waits to give us strength to do as he tells us, as soon as ever we ask him to do so."

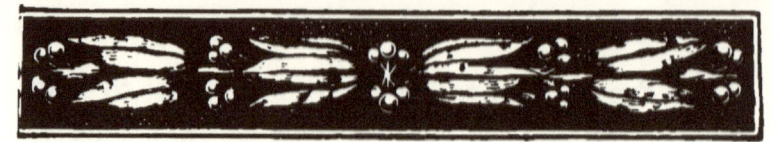

STORY OF THE SIXTH BEAD.

THE SPIRIT OF PRAYER.

"DO tell us, master Harry, whose picture to-day's story will be about," asked Jack. "Tom, and Johnny, and me has learned about ours, and we are glad of it, for the rest can't have more likely things to do than we have all got."

"Our Lord's Agony in the Garden is the next Mystery," replied Harry; "show me your pictures, and I will tell you which it is. Ah, there, I see, Ethel Rivers has it. You see Jesus is kneeling in prayer, and the angel standing by him."

"Dear, dear, how troubled he looks," said Johnny. "Is he in trouble, master Harry?"

"Yes, indeed, he is in great trouble during all these next five Mysteries."

"Somehow there seemed to be a good deal of trouble in the last five," said Jack, thoughtfully.

"Yes, Jack, because of the devil bringing in sin and suffering. They were meant to be Joyful

Mysteries as aunt told you. You know humility, and charity, and unselfishness, and obedience, and zeal don't hurt, unless our bad natures kick against them."

Johnny gave the little knowing nod which was always the sign that he accepted an opinion, and Jack was satisfied. The rest were still looking at Ethel's picture, when the Sixth Bead began its story.

" After the Prince had been to the Feast he did not begin to make a noise in the world, but lived on quietly at Nazareth, waiting till his Father should tell him what work he wanted him to do. In these days when young lads get to be fifteen or sixteen, they want to be their own masters, and don't like to receive orders from father or mother; and they want soon to have a hand in managing others, and to make their own opinions heard, and let people know what fine fellows they are. But the greatest of Princes had no such thought; he helped his Mother and obeyed her, and he helped Joseph, and took care of him when he was old, and stood beside his dying bed, and was as loving to him as the best of sons could be.

" It was not till he was thirty years old that the King called him to preach and to teach the people. It needs to learn a very long time, you see, before beginning to teach others. He went to preach, but he was very poor, and his mother had no longer a home to give him, for she could not keep the little house at Nazareth now that she had no husband to work for her. So the Prince of Peace had no home at all, but went about preaching all day, and then lay down in the fields or in a cave at night, or in any one's house who offered him a night's lodging."

"For three years he preached, and the people flocked to hear him. He was busy from morning to night doing good actions. They brought sick folks to him, and he touched them and cured their sickness; he restored sight to the blind; he made the dumb speak; he even brought the dead to life again. All these things he did to show the people that he was the King's Son, the true Prince of Peace, who had been promised from the earliest ages to save men from the Robber's cruelty.

"Great numbers of the poor believed in the Prince, and loved him, and gave their hearts to him; but very few of the rich cared for his preaching; for they said, 'He is only a carpenter's son, and has no learning; what he says cannot be worth listening to, and it is all nonsense to call him a Prince.' Only here and there a rich man, who remembered his duty to the King, and did not make a god of his riches, heard and believed the Prince, and so got back the right to the good home in the Best Land.

"You can imagine the Robber's rage all the time this was going on. He was very clever, but he could not see into people's hearts, only he could make very good guesses as to what was inside by watching how they talked and what they did. He had seen Mary at the well, but he was not sure that her child was really the Prince of Peace, for he was such a liar himself, that of course he never believed that either the good King or any one else could speak the truth. He failed in getting the child killed in infancy, and he watched his quiet life, and tried in vain to persuade him to commit sin. When he was a grown man he tried again, offering him all sorts of bribes if he would doubt the King's word, or pay homage to himself; but the Prince let him try all his devices, and never gave way to him the least bit.

"When the Robber saw how many believed on him, and got back their heart-jewel and their title to the homes in the Good Land, he trembled with rage, and went to the rulers and the Chief Priests, and persuaded them that this man was trying to upset government and religion, and must be got out of the way."

"Maybe they thought he was a Fenian, ma'am," suggested Johnny.

"They called him by some such name, and watched, trying to get him to do or say something against the law, that they might have an excuse for putting him in prison. They would have done it without any excuse, but they were afraid of the people, and of his twelve friends, who were always about with him."

"Please, ma'am, were any of them twelve Irish lads, for they would have taught the rulers they had better not meddle with him?"

"No, Johnny, they were not Irish. But they loved him very much, and believed that he was the King's Son, and would be the ruler of all the country. They expected he would take the country for himself very soon, and they hoped he would make them rulers under him; they didn't know that he meant to keep the new country on as a place of preparation for hundreds and hundreds of years, so that generation after generation of men should go on choosing which they would serve, the King or the Robber, and fight the old fight over and over and over again.

"The Prince knew that the time of his stay in the new country was near its close, but that he must endure terrible sufferings, and die a cruel death before he could return to his Father. It had come to the last night with his twelve friends, I should say with his eleven, for one had already deserted him."

" I'm glad they were not Irish men !" cried Jack. " I'd like to have punched that fellow's head !"

" On that last night he took his three best friends and went with them into the garden of Gethsemani. It was a dreadful thought that burdened his mind, for he could see all the past and all the future. He knew all that he was going to suffer for man's sake, and he saw a picture before him of how the most part of the people would refuse to let him save them after all he could do in life and in death. It was this sight of the obstinacy of man that made him suffer so very much ; also he saw all the sins that even his own children would commit—he saw your disobediences and mine, our acts of pride and selfishness and hatred, and as he thought of it all, he broke out into a sweat of agony, and the sweat was like drops of blood falling down to the ground. He might have fainted for grief and horror, but that his Father sent an angel to strengthen him and then he prayed more earnestly than ever, that if it were possible these sorrows might be turned aside, and each time that he ended his prayer, he said, ' But not my will, Father, but Thine be done.'

"Scarcely had he finished praying when the enemy's soldiers came to take him, guided by his false friend, Judas. They were so glad of the chance of taking him in the night, when none of the people were there to protect him. The three of his companions offered to fight for him—they were the only ones with him—but he said they should not fight, for all was happening according to his Father's will.

"Such is the story of the Sixth Mystery, and the lesson we are to learn from it is the practice of prayer. There is prayer of several kinds, some more pleasing to God than others, but it is the will of God that we should all pray. On this account the first lesson that is taught children when they come to school is to say their prayers. The little Connollys and Tim's little brothers are now learning their morning and night prayers. You can all say prayers."

"Yes, ma'am, those that they say in school."

"Good, that is the first and easiest way of praying. To say these prayers attentively, remembering that the great God is listening to your words.

"There is another way of praying which you will all learn as you get to know more about God and your own necessities, that is to pray from the heart, without a set form of words. St. Peter prayed thus when he was falling into the water, he cried out, 'Lord save me!'

"When we learn thus to pray from the heart, we can speak to the great God about everything. This is what He likes us to do. He is the best of Fathers, and He 'wishes us to be always asking favours of him. Thus hungry children ask for bread, sick children ask for health; and the good Father hears and gives them their wish, if it is for the good of their never-dying souls. Jesus prayed for us again and again, and His prayers were so good and perfect that they were like purest gold, and are stored up in heaven for ever and for ever. When we want to win straight to God's heart, we must say, 'Give me this or that, for Jesus' sake.'

"When our dear Lord was on earth, the people were always asking favours of him. One said, 'Lord, give me my sight,' and Jesus touched his eyes, and his sight was restored; another said, 'Lord, cure my sick child,' and the child was cured. Sometimes He made a person ask two or three times for a thing, for He had always in his mind that the people that came afterwards should take example by all that He did. One woman came, and asked that her child should be cured, and He pretended not to hear; she asked again, and He gave her a

6

cold reply, as if she was not good enough to have her prayer granted : but she asked again, humbly owning she was not good enough to deserve it, but reminding Him that He had such riches of grace that there was enough to spare even for such as her.   He loved her humility and her perseverance, and so granted her request.

"Now what I want you to understand is this— God desires you not only to say your prayers morning and night, but to be always in the spirit of prayer.   Do you think it possible to comply with this lesson of the Rosary Mystery ?"

" I am sure, ma'am, I can't !" said Jack despondingly.   When I am at work I be thinking about the drams, and the horses, and the loads of coal, and when I come up I think of my victuals, or of the lads, and what we play at, or of little Katy there, or mother, or father.   I couldn't think on to pray, except nights and mornings, nohow."

" Suppose one of the horses kicked you, and you knew that you were dying, could you pray then ?"

" Sure, ma'am, yes.   I should cry, 'God have mercy on my soul ; Jesus, Mary, Joseph, have mercy on me.'"

" Then you could pray when reminded by any danger ?"

"I suppose I could, ma'am."

" That is well so far, but I want you all to learn a simple way in which you can pray always, and be pleasing God every hour of the day, and yet not strain your young minds unnaturally. You like stories best, so I will try and explain my plan in a story."

" There were two children, called Sarah and Mary. Sarah was a gentleman's child, and went to a good school, and got great learning, and was sensible and clever. Mary was poor, and knew but little, and both of them were determined to try to serve God the very best they could."

" Sarah has the best chance," said Tom, who had a great respect for learning.

" Poor Mary may manage middling, but it isn't likely she can come up to Sarah," said Jack.

" She can't expect more than to come in sight of her," was Johnny's comment.

" Mary thought she had not much chance, but God had bid her to try to please Him, and try she would, though she only expected to deserve a very poor place outside the kitchen door of the Palace. When the Priest was speaking about prayer in the Poor School where Mary went, he said that the children should say as soon as ever they awoke, ' O God, I offer to Thee all I do and think and speak this day, in union with the actions of Jesus

6—2

during his life on earth.' The prayer was easy, and Mary got it by heart, though she could not yet read, and she tried to remember to say it every morning. At first she frequently forgot it, but at last it became a habit with her, and she said it immediately on awaking.

"Now in the King's Palace there was a great store-house of treasures, which the Prince of Peace had brought back from his travels on the earth. His prayers lay in one chest, like a great heap of countless gold. His acts of obedience, and love, and zeal, and humility, were like great heaps of precious stones. His sufferings and mortifications were like priceless gems, and He had won all for his children, and was saving all to give to them when their homes should be won.

"Little Mary was very like other children— like Nora, and Julia, and Ellen, and Jane, and Katy. She said her prayers morning and night as they do, and her Angel Guardian carried them to heaven; but they were not like common prayers, for on awaking she had offered them *in union* with those of Jesus, 'Oh God,' she had said, 'I offer to Thee all I do and think and speak to-day, in union with the actions of Jesus during his life on earth.'

"So when her angel took the prayer to the

Palace, it was immediately placed beside the golden prayers of Jesus in the treasury, and as it touched them, it became pure gold also, and was made into a crown that little Mary should wear when she came home.

"Mary's mother called her to sweep the house, to fetch water, to nurse the baby—Mary had to be very busy, and she could only think of what she was doing; but she tried to please her mother, and did her work diligently, and never knew what a lot of acts of obedience her angel was gathering up all day. She went to school, and learned to spell, and to write, and to say Catechism; she was rather slow than otherwise, and sometimes got kept in to learn her task, and otherwise punished; but she really tried to learn, and so made more acts of obedience. They all thought her stupid, and she knew she was so, and did not wish her teachers to think her better than she was; then her angel got an act of humility to put in his basket.

"At night when Mary went to bed, she asked herself, 'Have I pleased God to-day?' and her heart answered, ' You have done nothing that can have pleased Him, but by his help you have avoided being angry or disobedient; and the Priest says that if we avoid displeasing God, we may hope that we please Him, at least a little bit.' So Mary thanked God for taking such care of her, and went to sleep. Thus Mary's time passed, day by day, and week by week, and she never guessed that her angel took all these many acts of daily obedience and humility, and all her poor prayers and thanksgivings, and touching them with the treasures laid up by Jesus, turned them to gold and precious stones, and priceless gems, and made thereof a shining crown, and a golden harp, and rich furniture for poor Mary when her trial time should be over, and she should reach her home. And all this heavenly wealth came from the simple intention each morning renewed, ' Oh God, I offer to Thee all that I think, and do, and speak to-day, *in union with the actions of Jesus* during his life on earth.'

" Sarah had what is called a good head, and was well instructed. She knew the value of good actions, and resolved to practise them. The thing she least knew was her own great weakness, and that she could do nothing without the help of Jesus.

" When she rose in the morning she read long prayers. The King saw her devotion, and allotted her jewels for it. She heard Mass frequently, which Mary had no chance of doing ; she gave money to the poor, and to the Society for the Propagation of the Faith, and each night when she went to bed she counted how many jewels she must have earned that day. But she had forgotten the morning intention and offering, and the jewels were all of small value, though pretty good for a child.

" And the Robber saw these jewels, for she liked to keep them and look at them, instead of letting her angel take them in charge. He sent his people in disguise to her, to coax and flatter her, and at last he got her to think much of herself, and to count her good actions, as if they were her own making, and not merely inspired by the good Spirit of God. And as soon as this worst kind of pride entered into her heart, the door flew open, and the Robber got all her jewels, and carried them away.

" For a long time she did not know they were gone, for she was so full of thoughts about herself that she did not miss them, and she kept on saying prayers, and assisting at Mass, and giving alms, but as each jewel was given her in reward for the good action, the Robber seized it.

" At last a missioner came, and preached, and said all were great sinners, and Sarah was quite angry at his sermon, and the Robber laughed and clapped his hands to see her get prouder and prouder, and her Angel Guardian folded his wings and wept. Sarah felt very strange, and as she was going out, she was told that poor Mary was very ill, and had received the Last Sacraments. The angel begged her to go and visit her, but the Robber tried to keep her back. But Sarah was kind, and went to Mary.

"'Are you willing to die, Mary?' she asked, 'surely you must be afraid, for you have done hardly any good works.'

"'It seems strange to myself, miss,' replied Mary, 'that I am not afraid, for, as you say I have never done anything to offer to my Lord, and I must go as a poor beggar to Him. But somehow He has thought good to take away all my fear, and fill my heart with trust in Him. I don't feel ashamed of being a beggar at his feet, for the Priest says He has never yet been known to turn one away for poverty. I quite long to go to Him.'

"'But have you no sins, Mary, to make you afraid?'

"'Oh yes, miss, a sad lot of sins! The thought of them makes me very, very sorry, for his love ought to have made me determined against sin. How they got hold of me, I can't think, for whenever I found them I was like to break my heart, after all Jesus's love to a poor ignorant girl! I have confessed them all, and all are forgiven, but

I can't help going on grieving for them, because the good Lord deserved to be used so differently. They don't make me afraid, I only want the more to get to his feet, to tell Him how very sorry I am.'

"Sarah went home with a sore heart. Mary and she were the same age. Were she on her death-bed, could she so cling and confide in Jesus ? She knew when thus brought face to face with death, that something was wrong with her, and she went to the cupboard, where she had kept her jewels, thinking that the sight of them would restore her confidence. Alas, all were gone, and Sarah, the proud and self-righteous, suddenly became aware that she had been indulging a mortal sin.

"Our heavenly Father is very merciful. Jesus, ever seated at his right hand, is full of love to poor human nature. As soon as ever Sarah saw her sin, and shrank away in fear, the love of Jesus was poured out upon her, and He sent his light into her heart, to shew her all her sin, that she might make a good confession. Sarah came from confession weeping, and accounted herself the most unworthy in all the earth, as she knelt to receive Holy Communion, little guessing that even as the absolution was given, the King's guards entered the Robber's cave, and brought away all the stolen jewels, and washed them in the Saviour's blood, and stored them up for her in the heavenly treasure house, so that she was far richer at the moment that she despised herself, than she had ever been before.

"Now, dear children, you can without any difficulty learn the short prayer that was the secret of Mary's good life, and happy death, and joyous home in Heaven. Say each morning as she did, 'O God, I offer to Thee all I do, and think, and speak to-day, *in union with the actions of Jesus during His life on earth.*' If you can remember any time during the day to look up to God, and say of your work, or even play, 'For thy sake, O Lord,' so much the better, but at any rate adopt the resolution of the morning's offering, in memory of our dear Lord's agony. Let us say the decade in honour of his Prayer in the Garden, entreating of Him to teach us to pray so as to please the Father."

STORY OF THE SEVENTH BEAD.

CONTRITION.

" HIS evening's Mystery is the 'Scourging at the Pillar,'" said Harry, "who has got the picture?"

"I have, Master Harry," said Katy. "Our Lord is standing without his coat, and He is tied to a post, and the two men are beating Him." Katy's eyes filled with tears as she looked at it.

The children seemed in no mood to chatter as usual, and the Seventh Bead's story did not need to be heralded by a "hush," as some of the others had done.

"The soldiers dragged the Prince away to the High Priest's house. His friends ran away terrified, all except one, who was called John, and who loved him very much. Also another, called Peter, followed a long way off. There He was brought before his enemies, and witnesses were called, and swore all kinds of lies against him, saying that He had cursed, and sworn, and blasphemed, and tried to upset the government and the religion ; and all the time the noble Prince stood silent, answering not a word.

"The judge was vexed at this, and at last required him solemnly to answer whether or no He was the son of the good King. And the Prince replied that it was as he had said, and some day he should see him coming in the clouds of heaven. So they all cried out that the Prince had spoken blasphemy, and was worthy of death.

"But that judge had not power to order any one to death, so he said the prisoner should be kept there till morning, and then be sent to a higher judge. The soldiers that were left to guard the Prince ill-treated him all night long. They blindfolded him, and then hit him, and told him to guess who it was that struck him. And they spit at him, and ill-used him in every mean and cruel way. And all the time the Prince only needed to call to his white guards, and they would have taken the tormentors and torn them to pieces on the spot. But the dear Prince thought 'my poor people have need of so much patience in their pains, and griefs, and poverty, that I will win a great lot for them, and give it out to them as they need it.' So He let them strike him, and rail at him, and spit upon him, and never resisted them, nor said so much as an impatient word.

" When the morning was come the guards conducted the prisoner to Pilate the judge, and there all the lies were told over again against him, and still He made no reply, nor tried to defend himself. Pilate was astonished, and he said, 'Don't you know that I have power to order you to death, or to set you free?' and then the Prince replied, ' You have no power but what is given you from above, and they that have sent me to you, have done more wrong than you.'

"Pilate liked the prisoner because He was so gentle, and wanted to set him free. But the enemies had now excited the people against him, by telling them that He wanted to make fighting, and get them into trouble; so now the mob cried out, ' Crucify him, crucify him !'

" It was close upon a great Feast Day, and Pilate had made a custom of setting a prisoner free each year at that Feast, so he said kindly to the people, ' What, will you crucify your Prince, who has done you no harm?' and they cried with cruel fierceness, ' Yea, let him be crucified.'

"Still Pilate thought they would get into a kinder humour, so he ordered the Prince to be scourged publicly. Now you know that when a lad is sent to the house of correction for stealing, he sometimes gets sentenced to be whipped. This used to be done in public, and was justly accounted a terrible disgrace, it was indeed only inflicted on prisoners who were very insolent and unruly. Pilate could not have put a greater insult upon the great King's Son, than thus to order him to be stripped and flogged in public. When good people were working to get the black slaves set free, they showed pictures everywhere of the horrid practice of flogging them ; and it made all free-born and good-hearted people indignant against such cruelty, so that they gave heaps of money to buy up all the black slaves and set them free, and then the government made a law that no more slaves should be allowed in the British dominions.

"Only picture to yourselves, dear children, the good King looking down from his mountain throne, and his millions of white guards around him, and around the Prince too, though they were invisible to the eyes of Pilate and all the people. The Prince needed only just to look upwards to his great Father, and out would have flashed ten thousand shining swords from the invisible guards, and Pilate and the people would have had to kneel as suppliants at his feet. Indeed we can only wonder that the great Father looked on unmoved, and the reason that He did so was that He read all that was in his dear Son's heart.

"And what do you suppose He read there? Listen, while I try to tell you.

"When the Prince was praying in the garden, He saw in a vision all the sins that would be done in future years by men, and women, and children, as well as all that had been done. He saw most distinctly, and as it were nearest to him, the sins of his own people, of Christians, of Catholics. He knew that however large a pardon he should prepare for these, He could not rightly forgive them unless the doers of them were very sorry, and determined to forsake all sin. He saw that the one thing to melt their hard hearts, and make them renounce all disobedience and rebellion, was love; so He resolved that He would bear such great sufferings for them, and expend such an extravagance of his own love for them, as must compel them to love him in return, and for the sake of his love to repent of their past sins, and resist all sin in the future.

"For this reason it was that He stood meekly while the soldiers stripped off his clothes and bound him to the pillar, and the executioners flogged him till He was one mass of wounds and blood; He bore it all without a murmur, to soften our hearts, and to make them his own.

"The fruit that our Blessed Lord designed to grow from this stupendous act of love, is what we call *contrition*, that is, a true sorrow for our past sins, and a firm purpose of amendment. True contrition is sorrow for our sins proceeding from love to our Lord, with the real desire of Confession, and it is that which draws pardon at once from his gracious lips. Sorrow for sin because of the fear of God's punishment is a lower kind of contrition, though it also comes from the Holy Ghost, and, with absolution, is enough to restore the grace of God, if we have lost it.

"To make this clearer to you I will tell you a story I once heard of a boys' school. There were about a hundred boys there, and the oldest and cleverest boy was called the captain. At the time the circumstances I am going to tell you about took place, some new boys had been received into the school, who seemed to have a talent for leading the rest into evil; the master suspected these boys, but had no proof against them. Ernest, the captain, was an out-and-out good lad, kind, clever, and honourable, there was scarcely a lad among the hundred to whom he had not done many a kindness, some he had helped with their tasks, others he had saved from tyranny, one little fellow he had saved from drowning; when he got gifts from home he shared all his good things with the others, and he was alike the best at work and the best at play. But even he could not find out who began the various mischiefs.

"A friend came to visit one of the masters, and a private dinner was provided for him and his host in one of the studies. One of the new boys passed that way just as a maidservant set down a tray on a table in the hall; she was about to take it to the master's room, but having forgotten something she set the tray down while she ran to fetch what was missing.

"The moment she was gone the boy lifted the cover off the dish, and saw a roast fowl under it. Quick as thought he hid the fowl under his jacket, replaced the cover, and fled to his own room, where he assembled some of his choice friends, and they devoured the fowl together. Its loss was only discovered when the master had said grace, and raised the cover, and then the maid was questioned, and the cook was questioned, and no one knew where or how it had gone. All enquiries were in vain.

"The plums were ripe. The boys were never allowed to go to the garden. But the plums were all stolen, and plum-stones were scattered all over the playground, and yet no clue could be got to the robbers.

" The masters had the apples gathered in good time, and stored in an apple-room.   One day Ernest had occasion to fetch something from his bedroom at an unusual hour, and he noticed that the apple-room was open.   He remarked it to one of the masters when he returned to the school. That afternoon more than half the apples disappeared.

" The master felt that something must be done without delay, or the moral tone of the school would be hopelessly lost.   He consulted Ernest, but got no consolation from him.   It was very plain that a false idea of honour had got hold of the boys, and that they felt the master to be no longer their trusted friend, but an enemy whom it was lawful to despoil.

" The master proclaimed a solemn meeting, called them all to the chapel to unite in prayers for wisdom and help, and then held a trial in the large school.

" The roll-call was over, every boy had answered to his name, and stood in his place, the masters in theirs.   The head master gave a searching look at the faces around him, as he began his address.

" ' Boys,' he said, ' as I stand here among you, I

occupy the place of your parents, and their authority is delegated to me. They have cordially approved of the laws of my government, and I am bound to carry them into practice.'

"There was a solemn pause, in which no one spoke ; indeed, they seemed hardly to breathe.

"'You are all aware,' the master continued, ' that only great faults—sins against the Ten Commandments in fact, are punished by the disgrace and pain of flogging. It is a thing I abhor doing, or seeing done ; but at that or any cost, the vile and low sin of theft must be stopped ! I believe you would all recoil from the thought of stealing from a shop window, but to steal from me is a greater sin still in the sight of God, as all faults are greatest when committed against parents.'

"Another ominous pause ensued, but as yet every boy kept his own counsel.

"'Unless the guilty boys deliver themselves up,' resumed the master, 'punishment must fall upon the whole school. I shall be obliged to sentence all to the loss of pocket-money and holidays until the evil-doers are discovered ; unless, indeed,' he added, ' unless one should offer himself to bear the punishment due to many, which is not likely.'

"The pause was shorter this time, for whilst every heart thrilled with fear, Ernest stepped

7—2

forth and said in a clear voice, I will bear the penance, sir; I know nothing of the thefts, but I know that many others are innocent, and I will bear the punishment for all.'

"The master's lip quivered; he loved Ernest more than ever, but he had prayed for guidance, and he dare not refuse the sacrifice that might bring grace to all, so he only said in a low sad voice,

"'Uncover your shoulders.'

"Ernest did so, and as he was removing his upper garments you might have heard the loud beating of many a heart. Every boy present knew that Ernest's name was unsullied by one dishonourable action, that though in earlier days he had perpetrated many a mad prank, he had never been disgraced, and now he was going to endure the lowest punishment. They saw him prepare for the infliction, they saw the master's hand raised, and then they heard a bitter cry, and saw the least boy in the school, the one he had saved from drowning, spring forward and throw himself on his knees, exclaiming, 'Oh, sir, strike me! I was the first in the plum-tree, and I threw down the plums.' The master's hand fell by his side, as his heart thanked God for sparing him, like Abraham of old, the torture of his dearest child. Little Fred no longer knelt alone ; with one simultaneous cry of repentant sorrow every boy had started from his place, and was on his knees confessing his guilt.

"Ernest had resumed his coat, he also knelt by his loved master, and cried, ' Accept. their humble confessions, and, by your love for me, pardon their sin.'

"It was some minutes before the master could reply.

"'My children,' he said, 'do not again let the devil deceive you. The love of danger and adventure cannot make wrong right. You persuaded yourselves you were only making fun while you sullied your consciences with the crime of theft. I pardon you on all your honest confession, for Ernest's your captain's sake, but you must fulfil some penance to satisfy justice, and impress the evil of such conduct on your own consciences.

"'For a month you will forfeit a third of your pocket-money, and return daily from the playground half-an-hour earlier than usual.'

"Every boy was weeping ; the love of their captain had done what all fear of punishment utterly failed to do, and the spirit of rebellion was broken.

"Thus, dear children, as we kneel around the picture of our suffering Lord, and greet him with the prayer He gave us, and that in honour of his Incarnation, let us sympathise lovingly with his sufferings, and pray for a hearty contrition, such as He suffered to win for us."

STORY OF THE EIGHTH BEAD.

COURAGE.

"DEAR children," exclaimed the voice, as soon as ever they were assembled round the table for the eighth story, "look carefully at the picture, and note whom you see, and how he is arrayed.

"He stands, he, the Prince of Peace, the son of the great King, all weary, and sore, and bleeding, but dressed in a garb of mock royalty, a grand purple robe, such as emperors wear, on his bruised shoulders, a crown of thorns on his aching head, and in his hand a reed instead of a sceptre. The soldiers and the people mock him, and cry, 'Hail, great King!' They believe him to be only the carpenter's son, they have got Pilate to condemn him to death, and now they mock his misery!

"There are times when each of us get a little

taste of this kind of suffering, ridicule, and scoffs, and jeers, those that have borne such know how much worse it is than bodily pain."

"The other girls at the works do put bones among the sand that I use to clean my tin," said Polly, "both in Lent, and on any Friday, and they say to one another, ' We shall be having the Priest here with his cat-o'-nine tails, for you, Fenian, has been eating flesh meat.' But I let my tongue loose on 'em, and they don't gain much by their impe-rence."

" Why it's not more than a week ago," said Jack, " but the lads put me in an awful wax down below. It was dinner-time, and one had a tin plate, and another a little can. The one strutted before beat-ing his can, and t'other had a sack about his shoulders, and held the tin to his breast like—they were making game of our Priest at Benediction. I let fly and gave the bigger lad such a kicking as his shins are not likely to forget, the little 'un I rolled in the plack mud. I'll teach 'em to make game of Catholics !"

"Please," said little Nora Rivers, to whom the picture of the crowning with thorns belonged, " they are just as bad at our school now that Ethel does not go with us. They call us Guy Fawkes, and Fenians, and one day they got my new beads and broke them all to pieces. They are dreadful bad, ain't they, Julia ?"

" Oh yes, they do make us cry."

" And what do you do, my dears ?"

" We go home and tell mother, and she does say that we shall go to the Catholic school after Easter, only Miss Forbes, our governess, owes a good bit of money at our shop, and mother wanted to take it out in our learning."

" They don't molest me at my school," said Tom, " for I try not to let them know that I am a Catholic, and all our boys are strictly kept with their parents, so that they don't even come to our chapel, but if one of them should come, and get a sight of me serving at the altar, it would be all up with me."

" Now, dear children," resumed the voice, " you have shewn a few of the very small ways in which this kind of torture is inflicted, and how human nature bears it. Mind these trials you have recounted are very little ones : first, there is not one of us here who is worthy of respect ; if we know our own hearts and lives, we are obliged to own to God that we are good for nothing at all, and secondly, the things that are done to mortify us are but trifling. A passing laugh and jeer is about all that it comes to, and two or three of our companions are all that join in it. Look how dif-

ferent it was with the Prince of Peace. He was
the son of the King of kings. The man who was
judging him was a servant of the Emperor; the emperor himself was a servant of the great King. The
Prince was infinitely greater than those who jeered
at him; and look what his life had been—the per-
fection of truth, and honour, and love, and piety—
not a single stain on his conscience, or the possi-
bility of a stain, yet these very people whom he
had left his throne to rescue from slavery, these
slaves of the Robber, whose lives he was about to
buy with his own blood, these low, mean, degraded
creatures dared to ridicule his Majesty, scoff at his
crown, and make ribald jests about his sufferings!
Then consider how we poor undeserving creatures
act under these little insults, and how he acted.
One gives back taunt for taunt, ridicule for ridicule, sneer for sneer, and takes satisfaction in the
belief that her tongue has been even more bitter
than those that assailed her. Another gives blows
instead of hard words, certainly the kinder retort of
the two. A third complains, and seeks relief from
another authority. A fourth hides his colours,
hoping thus to escape the shame. Such is the way
of weak, cowardly human nature. Let us see how
differently our hero acted. Although at any moment he could have laid judge and jury, priest and

mob, prostrate at his feet, he never took one step towards self-defence. He heard their lies in silence, he bore their blows without flinching, he let them drag his clothes from him, and dress him up in kingly robes that they might insult him more deeply, and he offered no resistance. When they wove the crown of thorns, and pressed it on his head, so that the sharp points pierced his brow, and caused his blood to flow afresh, he uttered no reproach. He was busy still amassing treasures for his pauper children. He was heaping one act of courage upon another, until he should have enough to give to all the children of men, he was earning pardon for our cowardice by enduring its penance in wholesale measure, and he never felt he could bear too much for the succour of his lost ones.

" Dear children, whenever we are ashamed to do right, whether it is by owning our faith, or holding to obedience, or anything that our companions despise, and we know to be the will of God or the law of our Church, we are helping those who crowned Jesus with thorns, and when, by his dear help, which he gives so willingly, we gain courage to bear ridicule without flinching, to hear ourselves called Fenian or Papist, or otherwise jeered at, without an angry word or thought, we do a little, little bit towards repaying him for all he endured from the scoffs of the people. Also when we obey parents, or Priest, or teachers, despite the temptations and jeers of our companions, we give consolation to the Prince of Peace. I will tell you of a boy I knew under such temptation, that you may better understand what I mean by *moral courage*, which is the virtue specially exhibited in the crowning with thorns.

" This boy was a weakly child, but with a very strong intellect. At thirteen he stood in class above all the boys of fifteen and sixteen, and they were all envious of his talent. It was a large boarding-school, and many boys living in the town attended also as day-boarders—my boy was one of these. The big lads, who always tyrannized over the little ones, required James to buy for them in the town drink of various kinds, although there was a strict rule against the day boys bringing in anything, especially drink, for the boarders. Little James was weak in body, but eminently Christian. He knew obedience to rulers to be a great Christian virtue, and he steadily but gently refused to bring the liquor, or anything else. The big lads threatened him with all manner of punishments, but he remained firm. It was dinner time, the classes were dismissed, and most of the day boys and younger boarders had left the large school-room,

the masters had gone, and also the head boy, or
captain. Little James had got his books under
his arm, and was going out, when he found three
of the bullies stationed at the door. Once more
they offered him the money, and asked whether he
would fetch the drink, and once more he refused.
They then knocked him down, beat and cuffed him,
kicked him all round the room, and finished by
tying him to a bench and leaving him there alone ;
they even turned the key in the door, so that if
the poor child should get free, he could not get
home to take his dinner. Luckily for him the por-
ter came to put coals on the fire, and, finding the
boy, began to unloose his cords, questioning him
the while. But not a bit of information could he
get from James, for the same loyal principle that
withheld him from the act of disobedience, made
him resolute not to speak evil of others. The por-
ter was a very old servant of the establishment,
and did not fail to report what he had seen, and
add his own speculations as to the boys whose
cowardly conduct on other occasions made them
objects of suspicion on the present. However
nothing definite was found out, for James continued
perfectly silent, and was just as good-natured to
the boys who had ill-used him, as to any of the
others. Very soon they managed to find a lad of

easier principles, who brought them whatever they wished for. The consequence was that a horrid excess took place, which brought disgrace upon the school; the master had to have a public trial in the great hall, and the very boys who had persecuted James were sentenced to be expelled in disgrace. James is now a grown man, and a very distinguished scholar, and whenever he happens to meet a man who was at school with him, he finds a cordial friend and a warm admirer."

"He was a stunning good lad, and no mistake!" exclaimed Jack.

"He was that," added Johnny, with his oracular nod. "If I'd been in his place when they tied him up, I'd have had a bite out of 'em somewhere, that I would!" and he showed as dangerous a set of teeth as any dog could boast.

"And which conduct would give most pleasure to our Blessed Lord, to whom we owe our hearts, our lives, and everything, Johnny?"

"Oh, his, by a long piece, ma'am. I don't mean to say but that he behaved first rate; only natur is natur, and I couldn't have done it."

"Which way do you think the humble Virgin Mary would have acted?"

"Just the same as the Prince, ma'am. But then, you know, she hadn't got sin in her heart."

"Exactly so, Johnny. Then what is it that makes your nature want to do different to what Jesus did?"

"I suppose it is because of its badness, ma'am."

"Very true, Johnny. I like the honesty of your answers. Tell me now which is best, to give way to the badness of our nature, or to try to mend it?"

"To try to mend it," said Johnny, with some reluctance.

"Yes, truly. It is that we may see what is good, and try to do like it, that the Lord Jesus places Himself before us as we see Him to day, 'wearing a crown of thorns and a purple robe,' suffering all in silence, his heart as full of love as when He sat surrounded by loving friends. The courage to be able to bear insult patiently is very hard to acquire, but Jesus has lots of it ready to give us, if we ask Him for it, and persevere in trying to practise it. Now let us all make a strong resolution, while we gaze on the picture of his brave endurance, that we will endure patiently whatever comes against us for his sake. Men called Him a drunkard, and said that He kept bad company, and swore that they had heard Him blaspheme, and that He was trying to upset both government and religion, and He never spoke a word to defend Himself, nor wished a bad wish in his heart. We love and honour Him for this, do we not, and wish to give Him every consolation in our power?"

"Oh, yes, indeed we do," replied the children, one and all.

"Very well. Then the next time that people call us Papist, or Fenian, or any worse word, let us hold our tongues, and restrain our anger. Papist is not a bad word at all, for it only means that we are the children of our universal Father the Pope, whom we love with all our hearts. So when they call us by that name, let us say that we are very glad to be Papists. Also it does not hurt us to be called Fenians, if we haven't got the error of Fenianism, and are true and loving subjects to our good Queen. If they mock our Priests and our ceremonies we can't help feeling pain, but still silence is the best. The poor dear Irish, who might make themselves so respected for their fidelity to their religion, get themselves despised and hated for taking the law into their own hands, and fighting everywhere, and in some sad cases even murdering their enemies. If they would only look at Jesus, and listen to his voice—even when He was dying in agony He prayed, 'Father forgive them, for they know not what they do'—if they would consider the Lord Jesus, they would cease thus fiercely to take their own part. The Spirit of God says,

'Vengeance is mine, I will repay,' and when we take revenge for wrongs, we make God our enemy.

"Dear children, if we dwell on the sufferings of our loving Lord, without trying to do anything to comfort Him for them, it only makes our hearts harder. We must fight, not against them that trouble us, but against the anger and revenge in our own hearts.

"One more thing I have to tell you in relation to this day's virtue, *moral courage*. You have doubtless noticed that my nephew, Harry, is absent?"

"Oh yes, ma'am, we wanted to ask about him, but were afraid of interrupting. We do hope he isn't ill?"

"Alas, he is very ill, Jack, and he got his illness increased by an act of moral courage. You know he has made it his business for many weeks to fetch the little Connellys to school every morning?"

"Yes, sure," said Johnny, "it was his presentation work."

"Between the mine and this live a number of very rough lads."

"I believe you, ma'am!" was the rejoinder, with Johnny's sapient nod.

"Well, a lot of these lads lay in wait for Harry, and told him if he dared to pass by again on the

same errand they would make him repent it.
Harry said he had promised to fetch the children
while his strength lasted, and he should do it."

"First rate—hurrah for Master Harry!" cried
Johnny, and the others shewed their sympathy
by the excitement in their faces.

"This morning he went for the children. As
he was coming back the lads set upon him, and so
beat and bruised him, that it is very doubtful if he
ever recovers it. You know he has a dangerous
malady, and his father does not dare to hope that
he can live many years, but the violence which he
has received this morning, puts his life in present
danger. I am thankful to be able to tell you that
he has not uttered one hard word against the cruel
lads."

The boys were pale with agitation. Jack was
the first to speak, and his voice was hoarse, as he
said :

"Come on, Johnny, let us go and gather all the
Irish lads before they go to bed, and we will pull
them blackguards' houses about their heads."

Johnny half rose, but glanced timidly at the
lady.

"Jack! Jack!" she said solemnly, "have you
already forgotten, who it was who said, ' Vengeance
is mine, I will repay ?' "

" But our Master Harry—are they to kill him, and get no punishment ?"

" Jesus said, ' Father, forgive them, for they know not what they do,' and trying to act as Jesús did, Harry says also, ' Father forgive them—companions forgive them !' "

Jack burst into a flood of passionate tears, Johnny, and even Tom, broke down as well, and all the girls were weeping. It was some time before the lady even could steady her voice, and that gave them time to get over the first burst of their grief. Then she spoke to them with more than her wonted earnestness.

" Boys, you now stand face to face with one of your most dangerous temptations. Revenge is sweet to an angry spirit, and dear to the Robber, Satan, because it cuts us off from God. You have the greatest of examples before you, the Son of God, the hero of the human race, our God, and yet our brother. He is ever present with you, ever longing to see you patient and forgiving. You have seen how some such lads as yourselves have gained strength from Jesus to follow in His steps, and gain courage to endure and forbear. As you love Jesus the master, as you love James and Harry the humble followers, get the better of your resentment, and forgive the rough boys. A police-

man came up in time to see what they were about,
and he may prosecute them, but neither Harry nor
the doctor will appear against them. Before you
leave this room you must promise to forgive, and
use your best powers to persuade the other Irish
lads to do the same. We will say the decade with
deepest earnestness, to beseech our Lord to give
us this grace of moral courage, which we so greatly
need."

The prayers were answered in sobs rather than
in words, but the boys gave the required promise
as they kissed the picture, and moistened with tears
the portrait of " Jesus wearing the crown of thorns
and the purple robe."

STORY OF THE NINTH BEAD.

PATIENCE.

"PLEASE, ma'am, how is Master Harry?" was asked on every side by the children, as Aunt Margaret made her appearance on the next Rosary evening, and for once Christine's tongue was silent, for her heart was too full for speech.

"Harry is not better, dear children. He has to lie very quiet, and may not even be lifted up in bed. But our good Lord gives him great patience, and he has a smile ready for every one who comes to him."

"He did smile at me when I went to see him," said Jack, "but the sight of his white face was over much for me, and I got away as quick as I could." The ready tears rose to the poor collier's eyes as he spoke.

"Please, ma'am, did they break many of his bones?" asked Timothy, sorrowfully.

".No bones were broken, Timothy, but he was very much shaken, and the knocking about was too much for him. He was in bad health, you know, and could never run or jump as other boys did."

"It was a burning shame in those roughs to meddle with him. The men was a talking about it in the pit, and I can assure you, ma'am, it was all Jack and me could do with telling them about the Crown of Thorns to keep them quiet. A couple of 'em came to our house at night to ask a question or two more about the stories that the beads tell, and they want to buy some beads, and learn all about 'em."

" Very well, Tim, you shall have Rosaries enough, and you, and Jack, and Johnny, must repeat to them what you have learned. Then you will be little Missioners."

The boys looked much pleased, but Timothy had not done his commission fully yet. " And please, ma'am," he said, "will you get some big Rosaries for the men. They say their fingers is over big to handle the little beads, and they want to have the whole lot o' beads. They don't mind paying what is right for them."

"Very well, my boy. I will get them some large Rosaries, but five decades is quite enough for them to have, for you know the plan is to say first the five Joyful Mysteries, then begin again, and say the five Sorrowful Mysteries, and then again for the five Glorious Mysteries. Which kind of mysteries are we saying now, Timothy ?"

" The Crown of Thorns, ma'am."

" Yes, the Crown of Thorns is a Mystery. But what kind of Mystery is it ?"

" A very sorrowful one, ma'am."

" And what was the one before that, Johnny ?"

" The Scourging at the Pillar. That too was a sorrowful one."

" And the one before again, Jack ?"

" The Prayer of Agony. That was sorrowful enough, too, ma'am."

" Then how many Sorrowful Mysteries have we learned, Polly ?"

" Three, ma'am, and to-day's will make four."

" Who can tell me what the one is for to-day ?"

" I don't think any of us can, ma'am," said Ethel, " for it is was only Master Harry that knew beforehand."

" Then I will tell you. It is the Carrying of the Cross. Who has the picture ?"

" I have," said little Ellen Sullivan. " Here is the Lord with a great piece of wood over his shoulder."

" Yes, that is the picture. Now hear the sad story.

" The Judge kept on trying to save the life of the Prince, for he felt kindly to him, so he brought him out in the purple robe and with the crown of thorns, and he said, 'Behold the man !' as if he would claim their pity for his great sufferings, and he told them that he found no fault in him worthy of death. But they cried out, 'Crucify him, crucify him !' and Pilate said, ' What has he done to be crucified for ?' And then they said, ' He has done things against the law, and if you let him go you are no friend of the Emperor.' Then Pilate was frightened lest he should get into trouble with the Emperor, he knew it was unjust to kill the Prince, but he dare not refuse the mob, who were always crying out 'Crucify him, crucify him !'"

" He hadn't got no more moral courage than a mouse !" exclaimed Johnny.

" Wasn't he a big coward, ma'am ?" asked Jack.

' " He was indeed a coward to fear the people, and be turned by them against doing justice. But cowardice got the better of every one's courage that sad day, and the noble Prince was ordered to execution."

" If it was now-a-days, they would hang him, wouldn't they, ma'am ?" asked Tom.

" Yes, crucifixion was the degrading punishment then, as hanging is now. The cross was made of two heavy pieces of timber, and the soldiers who had orders to take the Prince to the place of execution thrust the cross into his arms and let it fall heavily on his bruised and torn shoulders. The Prince made no complaint at this fresh cause of suffering, but cheerfully began his toilsome journey up the hill of Calvary. Call to mind how the Prince had passed the night. He had had no chance of rest, dragged away from his prayer of agony to his first trial in the High Priest's house, tormented all night by the soldiers, no food given him, no rest, never a kind word in his ear. Then with the morning light he was sent to Pilate; Pilate sent him to his brother Judge, Herod; Herod sent him back again to Pilate. Pilate questioned him again and again, ordered him to be scourged, called him before the bar again after the scourging, had him stripped, and clothed in royal raiment, sent him out before the people, hoping to touch their compassion, questioned him again, sent him out again, and now loads him with the heavy cross, and sends him up the hill of Calvary. Who can wonder that his strength failed, and that he fell on the rough stony road, cutting his hands and knees, and suffering new bruises from the heavy cross which fell at the top of him!

"The Robber-king was there, invisible to the

eye, indeed, but inflaming the hearts of the brutal soldiers to the fiercest cruelty. He had seen the Prince before the judgment seat, he had seen him bear pain, and insult, and disgrace in heroic silence, he saw the heaps of good works, of Prayer, and Penance, and Courage, and Patience, that he was laying up in the storehouse above. He no longer doubted him to be the Son of the great King, and he knew that if he let him finish his work by giving his life a sacrifice to redeem men from the slavery of sin, that his black dungeons would be robbed of the thousands he had counted upon, and the courts of the good land filled with loving and grateful subjects. So he worked hard, knowing that so much was at stake.

" As the Prince lay almost fainting on the ground the Robber made the soldiers kick him, and prick him with their spears, hoping that their cruelty would wring from him at least, an impatient word, but when they pulled him roughly up he uttered no murmur, only toiled on again as fast as his exhausted strength would let him. Still the soldiers did not pity him, but they did not want him to die on the road, lest they should lose the excitement of the Crucifixion. So, when they saw a countryman coming along they seized him, and made him help the Prince with the cross.

, " With the help of this poor man, the good Lord
got on some distance further. His sweet Mother
Mary heard that something was amiss with her
Son, and she came to learn what was the matter.
Imagine what was her grief to see him thus suffering, and bruised, and exhausted, and going to his
death. She followed him closely to comfort him,
if that were possible, and his dear friend and companion, John, came also. You see them in the
picture, Jesus with his heavy cross, and the cruel
soldiers threatening him, and the Blessed Virgin
and St. John following, weeping.

" Surely this sorrowful sight should teach us a
lesson of patience. If the Son of God bore such
terrible pains without complaining, we should also
bear such as God sends us without a murmur.
Our dear Lord gave us the example at the cost of his
own blood and agony, and He did more, He won
for us the countless riches of his grace, so that He
has patience to bestow upon us in our every hour
of need. It is this that makes our dear boy able
to lie quiet on his bed of suffering, praying as he
does, 'Oh Lord, I accept all these sufferings in
penance for my sins, and I offer them along with
those of my Lord and Saviour to thy eternal
glory.'"

" But there is no one else like Master Harry !"
said Johnny, in an unsteady voice.

" You think so because you know and love
Harry, and he is the only one you have yet seen
bearing his cross ! You look astonished, Jack, for
when you came to Harry's bed you saw no cross
there—our mortal eyes cannot see them, but Jesus
and his holy angels see them plain enough. Sickness is a cross, and pain is a cross, and unkindness
is a cross, and dirt even may be a cross. You look
puzzled, Tim ; never be afraid of interrupting me
by a question, if you do not understand anything."

" Maybe the lads will laugh at me, if I speak,"
said Tim, blushing.

" No we won't," said Tom earnestly ; and Johnny
said in the same breath, " And what's the odds if
they do, man, laughing don't break bones !"

" Laughing hurts though," said the lady, smiling, " and it needed the Crown of Thorns to teach
us to bear it bravely. But you may speak quite
freely, Timothy ; those who belong to a Circle of
the Rosary are bound to love and help one another,
and never to hurt each other by deed or word, or
even by thought."

Timothy looked content. "What I wanted to
say, ma'am, is that folks think it disgraceful and
almost wicked to be dirty, and surely it can't be
wicked to bear the cross."

" Most true, my boy. It all depends on whose
duty it is to remove the dirt. If the women have

all dirty when the men come home, so that the house is miserable, then the dirt is a sin to the woman, and a cross to the man."

"Tim don't feel it half so bad to bear if it be his mother's fault instead of his," said Johnny.

"I don't want to put fault on poor mother, I'm sure," said Timothy, gently. "But I can't help feeling down-hearted when I come home hungry and tired, and the victuals isn't ready, nor the house cleaned up. It will come a bit easier now that I know it is something like what our Lord had to bear, and that He looks down kind-like at a lad when he is uncomfortable. But I have oft been in a very bad way about it."

"I don't wonder at that," rejoined the lady. "The Devil is ever on the watch to turn the goodness and love of Jesus to gall and bitterness. He knows as well as we do that the good God permits pain and sorrow, and poverty, and discomfort to give His children the opportunity of doing acts of patience and courage, which He stores up in heaven to make jewels in their crown hereafter, and gives them a lot more to them, so that to each of our little gains He adds a quantity out of the heaps that Jesus has won for us. The Devil seeing this tries to persuade us that we are very badly used when the crosses come, and that God is using us much worse than other people, and so he gets us to grudge against God, and grumbles, and frets, and hinders us of the good acts of patience and courage, often leading us to sin by angry and unjust words against both God and our neighbour. Sometimes, you know, the dangers seem more for the boys than the girls, such as those of fighting and revenge, but here is one which the girls must be on the look out against. When the house-work is neglected, and the fathers and brothers come home to a dirty, uncomfortable house, the chances are ten to one that they turn out again, and go to the public-house in disgust. Or if they stay at home they grumble, and scold, and possibly curse, and swear, and commit sins against God with their tongue. Or possibly they know that this is a cross, and bear it for Jesus' sake, offering it to God along with His patience in carrying His cross. But in any of these cases the idle daughter or sister is helping the Devil, and earning his wages. The sins of drunkenness or anger that the men commit in consequence, are partly put down to her account, and if they turn their discomfort to profit by offering it to their loving God, that does not justify the idle girl who has caused it. The Devil made the soldiers thrust the cross so heavily on the shoulders of our Lord, and it is he that makes idle women vex their husbands, and fathers, and brothers with dirt. By whatever means the Devil coaxes them to do it, they bring sin upon their souls by the neglect."

Polly was looking very cross. " Please ma'am," she said, in an irritable voice, "will you tell our Johnny not to kick me ?"

" Did he hurt you, Polly ?"

"No, ma'am, it is only aggravating me that he is."

" Don't do it, Johnny. You will never help your sister by teasing her."

" I don't want him to help me, ma'am. I come home from work tired enough, it isn't fair to expect me to tidy up the house. Mother ought to have it ready for us all."

" Mother's often bad in her head, and can't almost stand up, let alone brushing about in the house," said Johnny.

"Well, I can't do it no more than you can, Johnny."

" Couldn't we go shares, ma'am ? 'Taint rightly neither of our work, because of being out all day ; but when mother's bad we might make things a bit tidy if we both tried. I'll fetch the coal, and the sticks, and the water, if Polly will light the fire, and put the kettle on, and sweep up a bit. But when no one will lend a hand, I speak bad to them, I know, as I oughtn't to do, and then go and play with the lads, and leave them to themselves. And mother and Polly—but I won't tell tales."

" I don't mind telling, for I can't help it," said Polly, nearly crying. "Mother scolds me when I go out neighbouring, and says that it is along of me that Johnny gets bad ways, for I don't make a bit of comfort at home. And I say it is hard that I am to work in the house, when I have been slaving all day at the works, and I mean it ; only when I get vexed I say a deal more than I do mean, and then I have both mother and Johnny against me."

" Yes, and Almighty God besides, my poor Polly. But if you will try to bear your part of the cross with patience, try to tidy up a little bit, Johnny will lend a hand, and your mother will be so cheered up by seeing both your good-will, that she will have courage to try and have the kettle boiling at any rate. And her sickness will not make her so irritable, when she sees you are trying to help her. Will you try this, Polly and Johnny."

" Yes, ma'am," said Polly.

And " Yes, with all my heart," added Johnny, with his quaint nod.

" Can it be a bit of the cross when missus do scold one past bearing ?" asked Minnie.

" Yes, certainly, Minnie, especially if you are

doing your best to please her. Bear it patiently, and in silence, as Our Blessed Lord did, and you will get jewels for your crown."

" I do oft try to bear it, but sometimes I turn again and give her as good as she sends."

" Then you are helping the Robber, throwing away your jewels, and putting sin upon your soul."

"· Think of that," said Minnie, in astonishment ; " who would have thought of such a child as me doing all those things at once ?" After a moment she resumed : " I wonder what is Katy's cross !"

" Why, her bad headaches, to be sure," said Jack. " But I can't think what mine is, for I have not got anything to vex me."

" Then yours has not come yet, Jack."

" Well, ma'am, I can't say as I am in any hurry for it."

" I think my cross is Harry's illness. Is it not, Auntie ?" said Christine.

" Surely, ma'am, Master Harry's illness is his own cross, not Miss Christine's ?" asked Jack.

" A cross is often laid upon several persons together, Jack. Harry's illness is a cross to him-self, and to both his parents, and to Christine, just as Mrs. O' Rourke's illness is a cross both to Polly and Johnny. Crosses come to every one from

9

time to time, and can always be turned to gold if we bear them patiently."

"Miss Christine is a deal quieter since Master Harry was took worse," said Johnny, looking tenderly at the little sad face, usually so full of eager curiosity.

"Not like the same child," added Jack with an equally sympathetic look.

Poor Christine began to cry.

"Dear children," said her aunt; "Almighty God sends us all crosses just as we can bear them, and as we need them. Each cross is a mystery of itself, and if we take it cheerfully for love of Jesus, and do the best we can with it, we shall get more blessings from it than we can count. I have seen sick people lying in bed in pain, and as bright and happy as the birds in the trees. They have some of them been laid on that bed of suffering, for years, but they know *who* bore the cross for them, and they know *how* He bore it, and they keep looking to Him and asking His help and offering up their sufferings in union with His, and trusting to Him till their hearts are bound quite fast to Him, and they feel it the best and happiest thing possible just to do His will. Sometimes I have praised their patience and said, 'I give glory to God in seeing you so patient and cheerful, for it must be

very hard to bear such a dull and painful life as
yours,' and they have said, 'Oh, the life looks
much worse than it is ; it was a little hard at first,
but now I find it very easy.' They had submitted
to the cross so quietly that they had got quite
accustomed to it."

" They must have got a lot of jewels for their
crowns," said Jack.

"Doubtless they had, Jack. And they had
helped lots of other people to get jewels for theirs.
First they had caused many to praise God, then
they had made grumbling people ashamed of complaining, and so stopped some of their sins, then
they had won so much love and pity from others
that many had left their pleasure-seeking, from
time to time to share their solitude or bring them
some amusement, or if they were poor, some little
comfort that money could purchase. Thus they
had caused Visitation work to be done, and Nativity
work, and Presentation work, and Annunciation
work. For all these mysteries and virtues are like
brothers and sisters, and love to follow each other
about, so that where you see one virtue, you need
never be astonished to see any number of the
others."

"Please, ma'am, does Master Harry know all
the things that come out of a cross ?" asked Tom.

' "He knows that very many graces do come, Tom; but I don't know whether he has heard all about what you have just been learning. He was very sick the other day when you came to see him but he is better to-day, so if you like to go back with me, you can tell him all you have been learning, and how all the children remember him, and grieve for him, and so get a share of his cross. In the meanwhile, let us say the Carrying of the Cross decade, praying for patience to bear our own cross so as to win jewels by it, and for all those who have crosses to bear that the same grace may be given to them also."

STORY OF THE TENTH BEAD.

SELF SACRIFICE.

HE children had assembled again, but no one had any desire to chatter while they waited for Aunt Margaret. They had been a fortnight without a lesson, but they made no complaint, they were anxious as far as they knew how, to help their teacher to bear her cross. When she did come, holding Christine by the hand, they stirred up the fire to make a good blaze, and put a chair for little Christine close by her aunt, instead of near Katy.

"Sit by the fire, little miss," said Jack, "there's a cold wind over the other side." Christine couldn't help crying though she was trying to be cheerful, for that used to be Harry's place, just because of being the warmest, and now that Harry had carried his cross to the end, and gained his crown, all the children felt his absence more keenly than they wished to show. They might all have been cross or sulky, for they looked away from Christine, but the reason was that their eyes were full of tears, and they did not want her to see them.

"To-day," said the teacher, "we have to learn about the last of the Sorrowful Mysteries. Eleanor has the picture, it is the Crucifixion of our Blessed Lord. The mystery you last heard about was the Carrying of the Cross. Our Lord, aided by the countryman, carried His cross up the Hill of Calvary. When he arrived there the soldiers took his clothes off him, and laying the cross upon the ground, and stretching him upon it, they drove large nails through his hands, and through his feet, and then lifted the cross up and fixed it in the ground. You can imagine the torture of this hanging by the wounded hands and feet !

"But it was not enough for the cruel people to inflict pain, shame must also be poured upon the Prince in full measure. He was dying the death of a thief, and two thieves were dying beside him, one on his right hand and the other on his left. One of these was a very brutal character, and began to use bad and profane language, and even to jeer at the noble sufferer beside him, scoffing at him as if he was an impostor and a liar. But the other had got his heart touched with God's grace, and was quite shocked at the daring impiety of his comrade. ' Dost thou not fear God, seeing that we must soon appear before Him ?' he said, ' and we suffer only the just punishment of our deeds ; but this man has done nothing amiss.'

" Here you see at once the fruit of the Lord's Passion, as his sufferings during these three days is called.

" The silence and courage and patience of Jesus had taught this man to love and respect him, and believe in his being truly the Son of God. So he took his part with courage, and in reward for that he received the grace of prayer ; he who most probably had never prayed before. ' Lord,' he said,' remember me when thou shalt come into thy kingdom ;' and Jesus answered, 'Amen I say to thee, this day shalt thou be with me in Paradise.'

" You see, children, how much can be done by the grace of God in a few short hours. This man was an abandoned thief in the morning. Convinced by the sight of the Passion of Jesus, he confessed his guilt, and received some of the graces won by our Lord's Scourging, then he took the part of Jesus, and received the graces of the Crowning with Thorns, then he had grace given to pray, and to believe Christ's promise, and lo the whole life of a Christian was lived upon a Cross of Agony—Patience and

Charity came in the company of the Sister of Virtues, and the poor thief became by the blood of Jesus a Saint of God.

" Still the soldiers and the people who passed by mocked him in his agony. ' Vah,' they said, ' if thou be the Son of God, come down from the Cross, and we will believe in thee ;' and others laughed, and said, ' He pretended to save others, and after all he cannot save himself.' God Almighty was very angry, and Jesus knew it, so he prayed, ' Father, forgive them, for they know not what they do !' Their hearts were blinded by the cruel Robber, and they could not believe that one who was suffering a shameful death could be an Almighty Deliverer. The loving pitying Saviour would shield them from his Father's anger, even while they mocked him, and so he prayed, ' Father, forgive them, for they know not what they do !'

"All this time his sorrowing Mother stood weeping beside his Cross in bitterest grief. The faithful John was there also, grieving for him, and longing to relieve him. Amidst his hourly increasing agony, he remembered the desolation of his Mother, widowed and homeless, and about to be childless. He knew also how his dear friend John was longing to do something to comfort him, so he told him to take care of his Mother for him, and he told his

Mother to take John for her son. 'Woman,' he said, 'behold thy son,' and 'behold thy Mother.' From that time St. John took the Blessed Virgin to his own home.

"The weary hours wore on. The fatigue and pain and heat parched up the sufferer's mouth, and he said, 'I thirst.' The attendants brought him a sour drink, with an opiate in it, to deaden his sufferings, even they were becoming merciful now that it was too late. But when he tasted the opiate, he would not drink it, for he wished to bear the full weight of pain and grief for us.

"Then came the moment of most fearful agony. Long generations past, when first the Son of God offered to bear man's punishment, he submitted himself to endure everything that man had deserved. He would be accounted guilty and punished as a criminal; he would be accounted vile, and treated with contempt—all this he had borne and was bearing. But there was one thing more, at the thought of which he had cried in agony, 'Father, if it be possible, let this cup pass from me,' and that was the hiding of his Father's face. Hitherto in all his sufferings his upturned glance had always been able to behold the dear face of his Father in heaven. But as God had sworn to turn away His face from sin, and all the sins of men were now heaped upon the devoted head of Jesus, the Almighty Father was bound by His own word to hide His face. Then it was that the bitter cry was wrung from the holy sufferer, 'My God, my God, why hast thou forsaken me?'

"Yet not for a moment did the God-man flinch, not for a moment did he even think of turning from his purpose of bearing all anguish to save us sinful creatures. He bore the hiding of his Father's face as he had borne the scourge, the thorns, the cross, the nails, and when the fearful horror had passed by, he said, 'It is consummated,' 'It is finished;' as if he would say—my task is complete, I have borne all there is to bear, I have drunk the draught of bitterness till the cup is empty; the curse is borne, the blessing is won back again, the slaves of hell are set free, heaven's gates are thrown open,—it is finished.

"Then he looked up again to his loved Father, and his lips spoke for the last time, 'Father,' he said, 'into thy hands I commend my spirit,' and having said this, he calmly laid down his life. His griefs were over, and the Son of God, clothed in our flesh, hung dead upon the shameful Cross.

"Then the sun grew dark, the earth trembled, the everlasting rocks were torn asunder. The beautiful veil or curtain, which hung in the Temple to hide the sanctuary, was rent from top to bottom, the graves opened, and the dead came forth. Even the officer of the cruel Roman soldiers, seeing these things said, 'This must be the Son of God !'

" Then were the gates of the Waiting Palace thrown wide open, and the liberated Spirit of Jesus entered, and told those waiting there that their deliverance was accomplished. Adam and Eve, and the gentle Abel, and Noe, and Abraham, and Joseph the Son of Israel, and the Three Children, and Job, and Daniel, and Joseph the husband of Mary, and John the Baptist, and thousands of others saw the Conqueror enter, and rejoiced !

" And gentle souls came—Nicodemus and Joseph of Arimathea, and they took down the body of Jesus, and laid him in his Mother's arms, and they prepared to bury him, because the dead must be laid in the ground before the coming Feast.

" Such is the history of the tenth Mystery, the mystery of mysteries, the Crucifixion of the Saviour of mankind.

" The point we need most to fix our minds upon is the self-sacrifice of our Divine Lord. As he said himself, ' No man has power to take my life away. I lay it down of myself. I have the power to lay it down, and the power to take it up again.' This alone proves the Godhead of Jesus. No mere man

can take his life up again when once it is gone ;
neither can any man say, 'None can take my life
from me.' Jesus gave his life freely by his own
will, and he gave it for two purposes—first to
repair the injured glory of God his Father; secondly,
to save mankind from eternal death.

" The fact that a man could only be saved by
sacrificing a substitute, was of such vital importance
that God declared it to our first parents, and to
every generation afterwards. Cain and Abel had
to bring a lamb to die instead of themselves for
their sins, and to hope in the coming Saviour, who
should offer Himself as the Lamb of God at the
right time, and by the value of whose sacrifice
Adam, and Eve, and Abel, and all who were saved,
got their deliverance from the devil. When the
sins of men roused the just anger of God in the
time of Noe, and they would not repent, or offer
sacrifice for their sins, their God drowned all the
world except one family, and when that one family
came out of the ark, the first thing they did was to
offer sacrifice—lambs and calves—for their sins,
looking upward and onward to the Lamb of God,
who had promised of His own will to come in due
time and lay down His life for the forgiveness of
sins. When the children of Israel begged to be
set free from Egypt, it was that they might offer

sacrifices to God, according to His commandment, still looking onwards to the death and atonement of the Saviour, the anointed of God. All the Old Testament Saints found pardon by sacrifice, and the value of the slain lambs and calves, consisted solely in their being the foreshadowing of the death of Jesus on Mount Calvary.

"And we Catholics cling as fondly as they to the rite of sacrifice, only ours is offered in *memory* of the death of Christ, as theirs was offered in the *hope* of that death. Adam, and Eve, and Abel, and Noe, fixed their soul's eyes just where we fix ours, when in Holy Mass we commemorate the coming, and the life, and the death, for our sakes of our most Blessed Redeemer. In the Mass they say 'It is consummated,' in Holy Communion we make our hearts into a sepulchre to receive the body of our Lord.

"In the olden time the lambs and calves were sacrificed, not for any fault of theirs, for they were only accepted as sacrifices if they were perfect in health, and of the best kind. This was to teach the people that the Saviour would be good and holy, quite perfect as to His own nature, but yet to suffer death for the sins of His children.

"See with what great love He loved us. Some loving parents will give their goods, and their

time, and even their health for the good of their
children, but how few would give their life ! We
read a great many stories of noble hearts, but it is
only the love of God that can do and suffer what
Jesus did.

· " The work of salvation is complete, consummated,
finished, as far as Jesus is concerned, but He
requires us each to unite our feeble efforts with His
great ones to secure our personal salvation. It is
not that our work is worth anything in reality, it
is only as if a father was drawing a heavy load
and allowed his baby child to take hold of the rope
with its tiny hand. All the work is done by Jesus,
but He ever treats us as His own dear baby
children, and requires us to work with Him. He
does thus because he puts such a value on our love.
Thus He gave His own precious life for us,
generously, and without grudging, and He asks of
us to make our small sacrifices in return. He
wants to teach us self-sacrifice, it is the lesson of
this greatest of mysteries."

" Please, ma'am, how can we get to do that ?"
asked Eleanor, to whom the picture of the Crucifixion belonged.

" By looking very often and very attentively at
the actions of our Blessed Lord, and asking Him to
teach us, dear Eleanor. He is such a kind and

wise friend, that He will give us each something suited to our power. The great things He will ask of those to whom He has given great strength. I will tell you of one of these.

" I knew a very pious Priest, a Carmelite Father, and he had thought and prayed so much about the Passion and Death of Jesus that he longed to suffer and die for His sake, and he prayed continually for suffering, and even for martyrdom. His health became very bad, and he had pains of various kinds, and he was glad of them, and thanked God, he seemed always to be embracing and kissing his cross, and praying for more occasions of offering sacrifices to God. His only other pleasure was reading, and he spent hours, sometimes the whole night, reading what the Saints had written about Jesus. Most of these Saints had written their books in Latin, and when the good Priest read them, and learned more and more of the love of God from them, he thought what a pity it was that English people should not be able to read them also. So he began to write them out in English, working nearly all night long at his task of love. As his work progressed, his eye-sight failed. He was very anxious to finish his work, so he went to a doctor to ask for a wash for his eyes. The doctor told him there was no use bathing

them, for that both eyes were going blind as fast
as they could, and there was no remedy until the
sight should be quite gone, and then if he liked to
submit to a very painful operation on each eye,
the sight might be partially restored. The Priest
was getting an old man, and he did not expect he
should live through these dreadful operations
which required the eyes to be drawn forward in
the sockets, cleaned, and put back again, but he
nevertheless rejoined, ' Oh, God !' he cried, 'how
condescending Thou art. I was thirsting to make
Thee a present of something, and Thou acceptest
my poor eye-sight. Jesus gave His whole body
for me, and the more I can give to Him the better.
I offer Thee my eye-sight in union with His
great sacrifice, and my death in the operation that
will come if such be Thy will.'

"Cheerfully he laid aside his writing. Some
kind Nuns begged him to go and stay at their
convent, which was near a place called Lourdes.
' Father,' they said to him one day, "there is a
well near this which is dear to the Blessed Virgin,
and she makes many cures by its waters. We pray
you very earnestly to make a Novena in the
honour of our Lady, and to bathe your eyes daily
for the nine days in the well.' And the good
Father replied, ' My sisters, it ever rejoices my

heart to honour the Mother of God. I will make the nine days devotion to her as you propose, and bathe my poor eyes, but I have already given them to God, and it is His affair, not mine, whether they are blind, or whether they see. So the good Father prayed, and bathed in the well. Each time that the water of Lourdes flowed over his eyes the sight became a little clearer, and at the end of the nine days, he could see again quite well, and resume his work.

" Then he and the good nuns made a Novena of thanksgivings, and they praised the love of God, and the motherly intercession of the Blessed Virgin. But even as he thanked God he prayed again, ' As thou hast given me my eyesight, O Lord, please to accept some still greater sacrifice from me.'

" He was finishing his book, dividing his time between study and prayer, when he heard sad news. A terrible war had broken out in Europe, and the people among whom he had lived in his childhood were immured in close prisons, and dying of pestilence, and there were none to tend them. So he lifted up his eyes to God, and cried with tears, ' O God, I go in Thy name to these Thy perishing children, accept now my life, for I burn to sacrifice it to Thee !' And away he went to the land of the pestilence.

"Every hour was spent beside the sick and dying, he soothed their sufferings, gave them food and medicine, persuaded them to repent and confess their sins, and pointed them to the sure refuge of the love of Jesus. A few recovered under his care, but many died, washed from their sins in the blood of Jesus, and rejoicing that the pestilence had come to put them in the way of finding pardon and heaven. The pestilence was decreasing, each day there were fewer cases, and the Father's work of love seemed again drawing to a close. He was thankful for the relief to the people, but his own desire to give his life to God was more eager than ever. He rejoiced, more than a man who finds a purse of gold, when he felt himself stricken with the terrible disease, and as long as consciousness remained, he was thanking God for permitting him to die a martyr to his love. This has happened quite recently, so you see the great sacrifice of Jesus has lost none of its power to move men's hard hearts during the eighteen hundred years that have past since it was consummated.

"These wonderful virtues which flow out of the life and death of Jesus, steal gently into the souls He draws to Him. He begins his work with little children in the manger, teaching them to love God more than their toys, and be ready to give up little pleasures and possessions to their companions. The unselfishness of the spirit of poverty grows by slow degrees; by the added grace of Christ, the older child gives up more for God, bears discomfort, and even pain and disgrace for Jesus and his neighbour, patience and courage are added to unselfishness, and at last grace brings about the crowning virtue of self-sacrifice. The Christian, who in childhood learns from Jesus to give away what he does not really need, may have courage when grown up to nurse the sick in cholera, or to go to heathen lands to teach and to preach so as to win thousands to know and love Jesus.

" I don't ask any of you children to desire martyrdom, or any great thing ; you would overstrain your devotion by so doing, and most likely deceive your own hearts. It is enough for you to emulate the infant Jesus, fighting against your natural selfishness, and trying in all things to be like Jesus at Nazareth. In the meanwhile, let no day pass without looking lovingly on your Crucifix, and remembering the awful death your Saviour endured for you ; love Him for it, thank Him for it, give Him the consolation of seeing that you grieve over the memory of His pains, and then He will cause to grow up in your heart the grace of self-sacrifice in such degree as His wisdom sees you will have occasion for.

" While we say the decade of the Crucifixion, let us stretch our hearts wide to intercede for others as well as for ourselves. Christ died for all the world, for all sinners. Let us pray for bad Catholics, for those who, tempted by this world's advantages, deny their faith, and thus, as the Scriptures say, 'Crucify again to themselves the Son of God, and make Him a mockery.' Let us pray for all in mortal sin, for they live in danger of losing God for ever; let us pray for the Jews who in their pride and cruelty crucified Jesus on Calvary, 'not knowing what they did'; for the heathen who worship gods of wood and stone, and know not the Almighty Father, nor Jesus the Son of God, made man for us; and for our Protestant neighbours, who are separated from Catholic unity by the fault of their ancestors, and who may be only waiting for the light of true faith to return to the true church of Christ. Our dear Lord said, when preparing for his death, ' I have other sheep who are not of this fold; I will gather them also into my bosom, that there may be one fold and one Shepherd.' Let our fervent prayers be like good sheep-dogs to collect and recall the wanderers, that the arms once spread out on the cross may be filled with loving and faithful children."

STORY OF THE ELEVENTH BEAD.

FAITH.

THE children had assembled early in the afternoon, though the Rosary class was not to be held till evening, and they had brought flowers and moss in quantities, and the budding catkins of the willow, which children call "palms." Aunt Margaret was there, and little Christine, with their quota of flowers and evergreens, and the big table was covered with working materials, including long lengths of cane, and a child's hat-box.

"Whatever do you mean to do with the hat-box, Minnie?" asked the lady.

"Sew moss all over it, and make it into a basket to put on our little Daniel's grave, ma'am. There was a little lady stopping at the Parson's, and she made one last year to put on the Parson's child, and she told me how it was made."

"Oh, Minnie, were you so bold as to speak to the young lady!" said Eleanor, reprovingly.

" I wasn't bold !" said Minnie, indignantly ; " it
was on Flowering Sunday, me and another girl was
looking at all the graves, and we came to that one,
' Eh, but that's handsome !' I said, ' I'd like to
make such a one for our little Dan another year,
if only I knew how to set about it.' The little
miss was standing by, and she told me how to do
it quite free-like. I have begged the old box of
Widow Sullivan, and I had to go ever so far on to
the mountain for the moss."

Each of the children wanted to make moss
baskets, but Aunt Margaret pleaded that Minnie
should be left in possession of the device for that
year, she and Christine were going to make an
evergreen wreath round the grave of their Harry,
and a cross of flowers to lay upon it, with letters
made of wire, and covered with flowers, R.I.P.

Minnie's design was at once forsaken, and all
were eager to make crosses and to have the letters.
But at last it occurred to them to ask what the
letters meant.

Aunt Margaret smiled, " I was wondering how
long you would be content to remain in ignorance,"
she said.   " Each of you who wish for crosses,
must get two sticks of different lengths, and bind
the flowers and branches upon them.   While your
hands are busy with this, as Christine's and mine

are now, I will tell you the meaning of the letters, and you shall choose for yourselves."

"R.I.P. stands for some latin words, which mean, 'May they rest in peace.' We don't know when those who leave us to go to God arrive in Heaven; they have to wait in Purgatory till all their little faults and bad habits are done away with, and every prayer that goes up to God for them gives them a help. So, when we write R.I.P over their graves, it is a written prayer to God, and all Catholics on seeing it say the prayer over again, so that we win many prayers by putting up the letters."

"Our little Dan was oh so loving ! we all cried our eyes out at losing him ; but he was awful cross and spiteful at times. I wouldn't wonder if he had to stop a good bit in Purgatory. I'll put R.I.P., to get help for him," said Minnie.

"If we don't meddle with Minnie by making baskets like hers, she ought not to take our letters, ought she ma'am ?" asked Eleanor.

" Yes, dear child. The letters may do Dan's soul good, while the flowers can only proclaim our own faith, and so bring consolation to ourselves."

" Please, ma'am, tell us how they tell about faith !"

" Flowers are at once types or pictures of death

and resurrection. The Scriptures say, 'the grass withereth, the flower fadeth; in the morning they are green and grow up—in the evening they are cut down, dried up, and withered.' Last year our dear Harry was like a bright flower among us, and a little more than a year ago Minnie had her little Dan to nurse like a tender flower. Now both are cut down and withered as to their bodies. The flowers that grew in our gardens last summer are dead also; they faded in the autumn and died away, and the winter snow covered them, and the leaves and flowers rotted away. But the same kind of flowers are beginning to open in the gardens again."

"Yes, ma'am, because of the seed that fell into the ground."

"Just so, Eleanor. The seed fell down with the leaves and flowers, and lay under the snow. And when the sunshine came, and the snow melted, the seed swelled and broke, and seemed more dead than ever; but a stem arose out of its heart, and pushed upwards through the earth, and came out with green leaves, and then the bud formed, and now we have flowers again. Thus it will be with the bodies of our loved ones; God will call them forth, and they shall rise again, not like the exhausted withered autumn plants, but with freshness and beauty, and as newly formed by the hand of God, only just like what they were before."

"Shall we know them, ma'am ; will they be like enough their old selves for that ?"

" When you sowed your scarlet runners, Eleanor, was it cabbages or potatoes that came up ?"

" Oh no, ma'am, the scarlet runners have come just the very same as last year ; you wouldn't know the one from the other !"

" But the field that Farmer Banks sowed with wheat, that one just behind Widow Sullivan's, that surely came up oats ?"

"No, no, no," cried all the children, "it was good red wheat, for we gleaned in the stubble afterwards !"

" Very good. Then you see the field seeds come up the same, so you may be sure that the human seeds also come up the same. We shall see Harry and Dan again just as they were before, only all trace of sickness or sorrow, or fretfulness, will be taken away."

"Please, ma'am, will my basket, do ?" asked Minnie.

"Yes, it will do, only the handle is not firm enough. I will fasten it more strongly for you. Put a basin of water inside, and it will keep the flowers fresh. What flowers have you got ?"

"Mostly Lent lilies, for the daisy stalks are too short, and the snowdrops are over. I have picked all the wall-flowers that we have in our garden, but the red droppers have not come yet."

"The Lent lilies and wall-flowers look very well; get some fresh young twigs to put with them. See —I have cut you out a large R.I.P. in brown paper, sew moss all over it, and you can lay it on the grave below the basket."

"Please, miss, Ethel and Nora and Julia and Ellen and me have done the two pieces for the crosses, will you tie them together for us? We will cover our R.I.P. with flowers."

"Moss or evergreens will last better. I have everlasting flowers for mine, but I have only just enough, or I would give you some. Yes, there are a few, just to make a cluster here and there."

"Please, ma'am," said Minnie, as she finished her letters, the little lady did make a crown as well as a basket, "each of us has got a few flowers left, and there is just time before the boys come from work if we may make one crown together for Master Harry's grave. It will remind us of the jewels that our Lord did give him."

The permission was gladly given, but a difficulty arose, for each of the children wanted to take the best flowers out of their crosses to put into the crown.

Aunt Margaret objected to this, saying that it was so nearly the time for the class that nothing must be undone. The boys arrived while the discussion continued, and all of them had got a flower or two.

"Isn't mine a beauty, ma'am," said Timothy, presenting a fragrant white hyacinth. I want it to be for Master Harry, for his picture of the Infant Jesus."

"I've got a first rate red geraner," said Jack, "and a white one two. I fetched a Welsh woman a sack of coals for them."

"Oh, Jack," cried Minnie, "do let me have the red one; it is the colour of blood, and it can mean the Crucifixion, and let us put each a flower into the crown, as if it was the jewels that the Lord gave him. The last Mystery was the Crucifixion, and the red flower will mean Self-sacrifice, and he did like give his life to help them children to learn God."

"You can have your fancy, Min.; I am pleased with you for taking such notice of what you have been taught; you've been more thoughtful of late. Tim's white flower can mean the Jewel of the Spirit of Poverty."

"He had that," sobbed Christine; "he gave away everything he had. I got lots of things."

"He gave us each something," said Johnny,

" and I have got a nice blue flower like Tim's white
one. My aunt begged it for me. It can mean the
virtue that I got, Obedience."

" That is mine," said Christine, " for blue is
our Lady's colour, and she was the best at obedience."

Tom had got a sweet narcissus, and he found
some fanciful reason for making it mean zeal. The
girls had wall-flowers, and Lent lilies, and Aunt
Margaret taught them to bind wet moss round the
stems of the flowers to keep them alive. Then the
crown was made, and the rubbish cleared away,
and the Story of the Eleventh Bead began.

" The Blessed Virgin Mary and her friends laid
the body of the Prince of Peace in a nice tomb.
While they were doing this, the enemies of the
Prince tried to do more harm still. They went to
Pilate and said, ' That deceiver told us that he
should die, and in three days rise again. Please to
give orders that the soldiers watch the tomb, lest
his friends steal him away in the night, and then
tell the people that he is risen from the dead, and
so get them to believe in him entirely.'

" Pilate was cross at their teasing him thus.
He didn't like the work they had made him do, at
all, thus far, but he didn't want them to complain
of him to the emperor, so he said hastily, ' You

can put a stone before the door, and a seal upon the stone, and set a guard of soldiers; make it as safe as you can.'

"The tomb was a cave in the rock, and there was a door to keep out the wild beasts. When the body was laid in the cave they shut the door, and then the enemies rolled a very heavy stone against it, fitting it into the opening of the cave, and they put wax between the stone and the edge of the rock, and put a seal upon it. Then they set a guard of soldiers to watch, and they went away. The weeping mother and her friends also went away. They remained quiet all the next day, which was the Sabbath, and on the first day of the new week they went and took sweet spices, and scents, and fine linen, to put about the body, according to the custom at that time.

"As the women went, they said to one another, "How shall we get the stone from the door, for it is too heavy for women's strength?' But when they came to the sepulchre, the stone was already removed.

"They looked into the cave to see the body, but it was there no longer, only two of the good King's white guards were there, and they said to the terrified women, 'Be not afraid, the Prince who was crucified is risen, this is the third day, and you

know he said he should then arise. He has gone
into Galilee, go and tell his friends that he is free
from death.'

"They went to tell his friends. Peter and
John jumped up at once, and ran as hard as ever
they could to the sepulchre. John was much
younger than Peter, and he ran faster, but Peter
soon got there, and went into the sepulchre, and
saw the grave-clothes lying, but not his dear
Lord.

"Two of His other friends went out of Jerusalem
to a village. They talked together as they went,
and said how sad their hearts were about the
sufferings and death of their Lord, and how dis-
appointed they were at his enemies thus getting
the better of him, and preventing him from
saving mankind. And as they talked, a stranger
joined them, and asked why they were sad, they
said, 'Our Master is dead, and we hoped that he
would have saved us all.' Then the stranger said,
'You are foolish and ignorant, do you not know
that the Saviour was bound to suffer all these
things before he returned to his glory. You
mourn his death, but is not this the third day, the
very day on which he said he would rise again ?'

"They loved to hear him talk, he seemed so
well to know the mind of their dear Lord. They

reached the village and went into a house to get something to eat, and when the bread came the stranger broke it, and blessed it, just as their Prince had done at his last supper, and so by that they knew it was their Lord.

"And the women staid weeping by the sepulchre, and presently the Prince appeared to them, and called them by name, and said he would come to them again.

"Then all the Prince's friends came together in an upper room. They locked the door to keep the enemies out, for they wanted to talk about the resurrection. Suddenly the Prince stood amongst them. He said, 'Peace be unto you.' He shewed them the wound in his hands and feet, and the hole which the soldier's spear had made in his side. He reproved one for being slow in believing what he said, and he told them all to go away presently, and preach everywhere, and tell the good news that mankind was saved, only, he said, they should wait for the 'Promise of the Father.'

"Then the loving Mother and all his friends rejoiced, and were very glad, because his suffering was at an end, and his glory begun. And through all the good land there was nothing to be heard but harping and singing, and they praised the Prince as a mighty conqueror, who had stolen the sting from death, and from the grave, its victory. And there was music and singing in the Waiting Palace, and the glad souls went in and out. And in the upper room, and in the Waiting Palace, and throughout the good land the song was sung, 'Alleluia, Christ is arisen! Christ is arisen from the dead, and become the first-fruits of them that slept. Christ has arisen, and by his strength shall all the dead arise; Christ is arisen, alleluia, alleluia!'

"This Glorious Mystery of the Resurrection is designed to teach us faith. Our Deliverer has come, he has borne our punishment, we saw him die the death of shame our sins had deserved, and we saw him enter into the prison of the grave. He had said beforehand that he must enter this prison, but that in three days he would come out again. Now a man in prison can neither have freedom for himself nor for others.

"The poor disciples had suffered such grief that they had lost their faith in his promise, and they mourned as if their dear Master had left them for ever. But all was changed on the Resurrection morning, for lo, he comes forth from the prison, a King, and a Conqueror, and he carries away the keys of the grave so that in all coming time he can open it at will.

"Jesus rose from the dead, not for His own sake, but for ours. A man who would sow a field might perhaps first scatter a few grains in a sunny corner to test whether the seed were good. When he had sowed the whole field, he would keep looking to the little corner sown a few days earlier. Ah! there come the blades! the first seeds are beginning to shoot up; the farmer is content, for he knows that if the first seed grows, so will the rest, and in due time all the land will be covered with ripe corn.

"So it is in God's field. Christ was sown in the grave, in three days He rose again. Well might heaven ring with Alleluias, for His rising was the pledge that all the dead shall rise at the call of God, and earth shall be covered with a harvest of human life, every one the price of the death and resurrection of Jesus.

"We are such stupid children in God's school that we are continually needing to learn the same lesson over again. God has made all His works like spelling-books for us, that we might continually learn about Him. Every blade of corn that rises from the ground, every flower seed that makes a new plant, every fresh opening of the leaves tells us again and again 'Christ has arisen, and all who die shall rise again like Him.'

11

"This is the reason why we get flowers to decorate the church at Easter. The great Feast will be here directly, and you shall help me to prepare for it. The Welsh custom of dressing the graves on Flowering Sunday arose from the old Catholic habit of dressing the church with flowers at Easter.

"The Glorious Mystery of the Resurrection calls upon us to bear bravely the loss of our dear ones here. We look up to God, and smile through our tears, for we know surely that we shall meet our dear Harry again in the day of God's great harvest.

"Look forward, dear children, in glad trust to the Resurrection, but don't forget your resurrection dress. St. John saw in a vision the risen Saints assembled around the Lord, and every one of them was clothed in white garments, and the Angel told him that they had 'washed their robes, and made them white in the blood of the Lamb.'

"It is for this very reason that all Catholics are required to go to Confession at Easter. The Church is a wise and loving Mother; her own eyes are fixed on the glorious truth of the Resurrection, and as she looks around upon her children, and sees them working and struggling, suffering, and sinning on every side, she cries, 'O, children, you must one day die, but you will rise from the dead.

You will rise with the same bodies which die, and if your souls are stained with mortal sin, you will rise with them stained, and that stain is the Robber's mark, by which he will claim his own. Death is among you, children; each Easter some places are made vacant by him, that were full last year. Hasten, children, wash your stained garments, hate the sins that killed Jesus, confess them, wash in His blood. Then if death comes suddenly in the coal pit, or by the iron forge, or in the small-pox, or wasting fever, the poor body goes peaceably, like Jesus, into the grave, to rise again in glory and beauty, washed in His blood, and clothed in His virtues, when God proclaims the Resurrection.

"All the joys of this Glorious Mystery are the free gift of Jesus to every Christian child. When the friends of Jesus knew that He had risen, they were glad, but His enemies were very sorry. The Robber is called the Father of lies, for he dearly loves lying, and teaches children, and men, and women, to speak and act falsely, whenever he can. He put a great big lie into the soldier's mouths, and paid them money for telling it. 'Say,' said he, 'His friends came by night, and stole Him away.' So the ignorant, idle people who made up the mob at that time heard that the body of Jesus had been stolen, and so they lost the know-

11—2

ledge of the resurrection, and with it, all faith in God.

"Dear children, were I to tell you that the queen was coming here, or that a tunnel was going to be made through Machen mountain, you would believe me because you have always known me to speak the truth, and because you love me. These same reasons hold good, and in much greater force, for believing all that God teaches us by His Word in the Church. He said that disobedience would bring death, and death came, and that death would have been eternal upon us all, had not Christ died, and so borne the great death for us. He said that obedience would bring life. Christ obeyed, and lo, eternal life is offered to all. He said that Christ would rise from the dead, and all should likewise rise in due time : and Christ has arisen, so we know that our resurrection is sure. The Robber knows that by believing in the true God, and in Jesus Christ whom He has sent, we get eternal life, pardon of our sins, cleansing in His blood, virtues wherewith to adorn our souls, courage to resist the devil's temptations, final victory over the enemies of our souls, and a home with God in heaven ; so he tries his every art to prevent our believing. We cannot believe of ourselves, Faith is a gift of God, and we should value it more than

ever such a grand property. It is God who gives
Faith, and it is God who enables us to keep it.
Let us say the decade in Thanksgiving for our
Faith, and praying Him to preserve it to us."

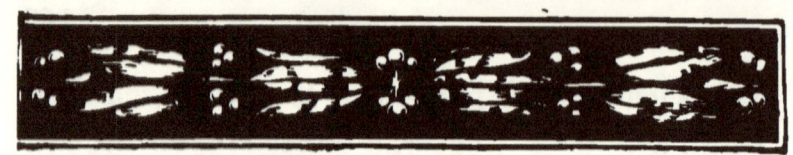

STORY OF THE TWELFTH BEAD.

HOPE.

" HOSE picture is the story about to-day, I wonder !" said Jack. "There are only four left. Let us see them, little ones."

Julia, Jane, and little Pat turned up their pictures, but Polly disdained any notice of the request that had been made to the "little ones."

"Julia's looks most likely : it is our Lord going up among the clouds ; Jane's has got a lot of folks together with lights on their heads, and Pat's is surely the blessed Virgin with lots of angels about her !"

He was just going to enquire for the fourth remaining picture, when he heard the words, "Listen children !" so he stopped speaking, and disposed himself to attend to the story of the twelfth Bead.

"The Prince of Peace had seen and pitied all the grief and all the doubts of his poor friends at

the time of his death, and while he lay in the
tomb, and so when he came out of that gloomy
prison, he waited a time in the new country to
comfort and reassure his Mother and his friends,
and establish in their hearts a firm hope of the
good things that he intended to do for them, but
which they could not see with their eyes.

"As soon as ever his Mother saw him she was
quite consoled. She could not help grieving for
his pain, but as soon as she saw that he was free
from pain, and from prison, that his toilsome work
was done, and he was ready to go back to his
Father, she was quite happy. There was no selfishness in her heart, and dearly as she loved her noble
Son, she was willing to lose him from her side, so
that she knew he was happier and better off than
with her. His will was her will, and whatever he
wished she wished.

"But his friends were still sad, for they had so
often heard him say that he would redeem all his
people, forgive their sins, lock the Robber up so
that he could no more tempt to sin, and give his
friends thrones and possessions in the Good Land.
And after saying all this he had died without gain-
ing any victory at all, and he would leave them in
the new country, poorer, more harassed, and more
miserable than ever. Poor people ! they were just

like children, who expect everything to be done the
very moment, and cry and pout because the flowers
do not come the very day the seed has been put
into the ground.

"Some people get very angry with children when
they are thus unreasonable ; but the Prince of Peace
only pitied his friends very much in their disap-
pointment, and stayed yet many weeks away from
his Father and the Good Land, in order to teach
them both to *hope* for his promises, and patiently
to *wait* for them.

"He joined those who conversed together, and
gently explained to them that the victory could
not come before the battle was fought, and that all
the bright hopes that he had promised were sure,
though they were yet far off. He came to their
religious meetings, he came to them at work, and
always he tried to teach them that the homes were
sure, the prize secured, but that each one must
fight as he had done, and suffer and repent, and
hope and wait—that the field must be watched,
the birds scared away, that the rains must descend,
and the winds must blow, and the sun must shine
—day by day, and week by week, and only after
long patience could the harvest be reaped.

"It was hard for them to accept this teaching,
for in their eager impatience they wanted the

Prince to reign immediately, and have the Robber punished. The Prince reasoned with them tenderly, and told them they must all go out as sowers with good seed; they must teach men in all parts of the country to love the Prince, and call upon him for help, and resist the Robber, and only after they had taught all that could they expect their reward. And he promised them that the Father would send to them his Spirit, to comfort and to strengthen, and to teach them all things as soon as ever the Prince should go back to the home of the Father.

" His friends clung to him more than ever, and he promised to visit them continually, even after he should have gone home. He could be in all places at the same time, so he said he would live among them and come into their hearts, only he must come in disguise as long as ever the Robber continued fighting for the new country. They smiled and took courage when he gave them these promises, and followed him jealously as he walked, for they were always in dread of his leaving them. They came at last to a mountain, and then he stopped, and told them again that he would be ever with them, and he breathed on them, and told them to go and preach, and teach all nations, baptizing them in the name of the Father and of the Son and of the Holy Ghost. And while he was still speaking the heavens opened, and he entered into a bright cloud and disappeared from their sight. They looked up eagerly, longing that he would come back again, and as they looked some of the white guards came and said, 'Why do you gaze into Heaven? In due time the Prince of Peace will come down again, just in the very way in which he has gone up.'

"So they knew it was one of the far-off hopes, and they went back to the town to wait for the Comforter, whom the Father had promised to send after the return of the Prince. They were very weak, always living in fear of enemies, and dreading every temptation, thinking that they should not be able to persevere in loving and serving the good King now that the Prince was no longer with them. They reminded one another from day to day of the sweet promise of their Lord, 'I will be with you all days,' and of the beautiful hope of the heavenly home, and the Prince's sweet Mother reminded them; that hope was the one thing that kept their hearts from breaking.

"The Prince's poor friends were low-spirited because they could see such a very little way; but there were some who knew how glorious a mystery this ascension of the Prince was.

"The people in the Waiting Palace were now

free, but what was the use of freedom to home-sick people when the gates into their country were fast barred. But the bright cloud that hid the Prince from the eyes of his poor friends sailed to the Waiting Palace, so that all there could get into it. Adam and Eve, and Abel, and Noe, and the patient Job, and the brave Daniel, and John the Son of Elizabeth, and Joseph the foster father of the Prince, and all the little babies under two years old, who had been murdered by the Robber's judge, and millions of other babies, and of men and women who had loved the good King, and obeyed him, and called upon the Prince of Peace ; all these got into the bright cloud, and the Prince took them to the glorious gates of the Best Land. And as they went upwards they sang with loud voices, ' Lift up your heads, ye gates, and be ye lifted up, ye everlasting doors, that the King of Glory may come in.'

" They sang ' Alleluia' when the gates opened, and all the white guards sang ' Alleluia,' and the Prince was clasped in his Father's arms, and all the Good Land echoed with rejoicings.

" This return to heaven of our Blessed Lord is called the Ascension. It is the second of the Glorious Mysteries, for it made perfect the joy of all the souls who had died before Jesus, and it

secures the hope of all who shall die after him.
Jesus made himself our pattern and example—as
he died we must die, as he rose again so shall we
rise, as he ascended into heaven so may we hope
to ascend, only there is one difference—we are sure
of the death and rising again, that is independent
of our will, but our ascending into heaven after
our resurrection depends on whether we belong to
Jesus or to the Devil. After the great resurrection
each must follow his chosen master.

"The virtue taught by this mystery is hope. It
was hope that raised the spirits of the desponding
disciples, the hope that Jesus would be ever with
them, though disguised—the hope that he would
come again at last, visibly to their longing eyes, in
the clouds of heaven, accompanied by angels and
archangels, and the spirits of the just whose bodies
still lay in the tombs.

"All of us have many reasons for hoping in God
in all our trials. He has promised to help us, that
is one reason ; He is supremely good, that is another
reason ; and He is all powerful, that is a third
reason. God is pleased when we hope in Him, and
He never fails those that do so."

"Connolly's wife said she hoped some way would
be found of getting the children to school now

that dear Master Harry is gone, but it does not seem likely," said Polly.

" Likely and unlikely has very little to do with God," said the lady. " If Mrs. Connolly prays to Him, He will find the way."

"Please, ma'am, it ain't so unlikely neither," said Timothy. "Who do you think was at our chapel on Good Friday, and crying like a good one at all the Priest told of the sufferings and death of our Lord? It was one of them very lads as set on Master Harry! And he was there again, and two or three more with him on Easter evening, I saw them from the singing gallery."

" Were they up to any larks, Tim?" asked Jack, with a severe look.

"Not to any at all, man. They behaved as quiet as could be, only for not knowing just when to kneel down. It's my belief as some of them lads had never been in a place of worship before. That set spends Sunday squirrel-hunting, or playing at Aunt Sally, or such like."

" Well now, boys, I will tell you a secret, but mind you must promise not to speak of it." All promised, so the lady continued.

"One of those lads got a bad accident when squirrel-hunting, his parent dare not send for the doctor, and there is no other within six miles as you know, but they sent a man off to summon him, nevertheless. Our doctor passed in the meanwhile, and seeing a crowd about the house he walked straight in, and found the lad bleeding very badly. None of them could look him in the face, but he did all for the lad that he could have done for any of you. Nothing was said at the time, but to-day the boy came to him, and asked pardon with tears for their ill-usage of Harry; he said they did not know he had anything the matter with him, and they have all been uncomfortable in their minds ever since. They have given a promise never again to molest any of our little ones in coming to our school, so you see Mrs. Connelly will not go without her reward for hoping in God. I trust you Catholic boys will look well to your ways, for if you behave rudely to these poor ignorant lads, you will drive them back to their paganism, and now they are certainly attracted to the religion of Jesus. You must be civil to them, and pray for them."

"That we will, ma'am. I am glad Connellys are keeping on at school, for Katy says they get on nicely at Catechism, and the White's too. You will have to make another Rosary Circle soon, for ours is full, and there's ever so many are asking about belonging to a Circle."

" All in good time, Jack. Let me get you fifteen to know thoroughly well what you are about first.

" A certain family wanted to go to America, and when they talked about it their next door neighbours wanted to go too. Fortman and his wife were hard-working people, and brought up their children to be industrious and to serve God; they had a large family, and they found it very very difficult to save money enough to pay the passage for all. Jones was fond of drink, and his wife loved gay clothes, so no one believed that they could ever save enough to take themselves and their two children across the seas.

" A bad time came. There was an accident in the coal mine, and all the colliers were thrown out of work. Only the two lads, John Fortman and Dick Jones, had got some kind of a place about the clerks' houses, by which they earned a small sum weekly, but that was too little to keep themselves, and could be no help at all for their families.

" Fortman and his wife looked the difficulty in the face, if they now began to live on the money saved for America, they must give up all thought of ever going there. There could be no work about the old home for six months to come, and no chance in any way. They counted the money, and found that by using that and selling their furniture, they could raise enough to take all the family except John. So when John came home at night they told him all about it, and said that if he would stop quietly and do as well as he could, they would send him money to follow them as soon as ever Fortman got work in America. John was a brave lad, he believed his father, because he had never heard him tell a lie, and he knew that he was clever, and industrious, and kind, and would be sure to have both the power and the will in time to do well for his son. So he answered his parents cheerfully, and said that he would hope in them and in God, and keep a good heart.

"Jones went about grumbling and complaining, and so teased the masters, and the gentry, and the people in the town some miles off, that at last they agreed to give him something to take him and his wife to America. He said it didn't signify taking Dick, for as Fortman had left his lad at home to keep himself till he could send him a pass to follow him, why Dick might as well do the same. So the Fortmans and Joneses sailed in one ship, and the boys staid to work for their bread at home.

"They got leave to sleep in the stables, for now that the pit was not working, very few horses were kept. The small wages scarcely procured them bread and a bit of tea—other comforts such as sugar, or butter, or cheese, they never had a chance of. Dick cried bitterly for cold and dreariness many a night, but though John suffered just as much, he did not cry, for he said, 'If we keep up our hearts a little while our fathers will send for us, and then we shall have as good a home as we could wish.' But Dick answered, amid his sobs, 'Father never kept his word yet, and he likes drink so much that he won't be able to save any money, besides, he is no great hand at getting it.' Poor Dick, you see, could neither hope in his father's promise, nor in his love, nor in his power.

" John was sent with the letters to the post, and as he went along the road he saw something lying in the mud. He picked it up, and how his heart leaped when he saw that it was a purse, and that there was money enough in it to take him to America, and to buy him a new suit of clothes to go in. But in a few minutes he remembered that it would be a dishonest act to take it, and that his father would give him no welcome if he came to him by dishonest means, so he carried the purse at once to his master, and he took it gladly, for the owner was already enquiring about it. He only gave John a shilling, and the thing was soon forgotten. Even Dick said little about it, for he thought John the biggest fool he had ever heard of.

12

John went whistling about his work, for the months were fast passing, and though he was getting very ragged, he thought, 'Father knows that I am short of victuals, and my clothes must be wearing out. I know he won't forget, and he is so industrious, and so kind, that he can't be very long in getting the money.'

"One day Dick was sent to the post instead of John. The mistress gave him a letter, and said, 'Take great care of that, for there is a bank note in it.' Dick set off, but he never came back again. When evening came the master called for him, and he could not be found ; he then enquired who had seen him, and learned the errand that had been entrusted to him. He went immediately to the post office, but he had not been there. First thing in the morning he went to the town, and enquired of the police. Poor Dick was in the lock-up, he had been taken for trying to change the ten pound note which he could give no reason for having in his possession. A policeman had already been sent up the valley to make enquiries about him. So Dick was tried for theft, and sentenced to prison ; but when his judges saw his half-starved hopeless face, they pitied him, and sent him to a reformatory school, instead of to prison, where he would be kept in food and clothing for five years, and taught a trade, only he would have hard work and very little pleasure all that time. John had to wait twelve months instead of six, and he had to bear a great deal of cold and hunger, but he never lost his courage, for his father had promised, and he knew him to be both capable and loving.

"At last he got his reward. The longed-for letter came. Work had not been quite so easy to find as they expected, but they had got it now, and a snug home, and good fire, and loving welcomes awaited John. There was money to buy him clothes and food at once, and a pass to take him his whole journey besides.

" Now you see the difference between these two boys was that the one had a well-founded hope, and the other had none ; and that is just the difference between those who belong to God, and those who belong to the devil. We hope in God in every difficulty, because of His promise, His goodness, and His power. He loves us to hope in Him. Let us say the decade, thanking Him for the hope that He so generously gives us, and praying Him to strengthen it in us ever more and more."

12—2

STORY OF THE THIRTEENTH BEAD.

ZEAL FOR SOULS.

"JANE'S picture is such a curious one, ma'am; wc can't guess by no means what it can be about," said Jack, as the lady took her seat in the class room.

"The Bead will tell its own story," she replied. "See the friends of the Prince are all assembled together, and tongues of fire are on their heads! Listen to the story."

"After the Prince was gone his friends had only the hope that he had given them to save their hearts from breaking. He had told them to wait at Jerusalem for the 'Promise of the Father,' and when that had come, to begin to preach and to teach. They gathered themselves together in that upper chamber that they had hired, and prayed, and hoped, and wondered, and waited.

"It was another great Feast at Jerusalem, and

a vast number of people were gathered together from all parts of the world, wearing different dresses, and speaking different languages. Some had come to worship the great God, but most had come from curiosity; and as the poor disciples passed through the street they heard people jabbering all kinds of languages, and it made them feel more timid than ever, for you know they were only poor men, fishermen, and clerks, and such like, and had little or no learning.

"They met together on that Sunday in their upper room to pray to Jesus in heaven, and beg him to send the Comforter. It frightened them so to think of having to go out to preach when they didn't know how to make a sermon at all!

"All at once, while they were praying, they heard a great noise, as if a strong wind were rushing into the house, and they saw fiery tongues in the air, each seeming as if it was split, and both sides in flames, and these tongues came and sat upon each of them, and instantly they were filled with new life, the Spirit of God entered into them, and they began to speak with the wisdom of Almighty God. They who had had no words to string together before, began to preach like the best instructed men; they could even speak other languages, as French, and German, and all kinds of tongues as

the men of different nations were speaking in the
streets. The preaching they had so feared was
now quite easy to them.

"They went out of their upper chamber, eager
to begin their work. They spoke to the people
standing about in the streets, and it became noised
abroad immediately that a great miracle had taken
place. Then the peeple ran together from all parts
of Jerusalem, and they questioned the Disciples,
and whatever language they spoke to them in the
Disciples answered in the same tongue. The
people were amazed, and exclaimed, 'Surely all
these men are from Galilee, yet we hear them speak
in our own tongue ! We are here Parthians, and
Medes, and Elamites, and inhabitants of Mesopo-
tamia, Judæa and Cappadocia, Pontus and Asia,
Phrygia and Pamphylia, Egypt, and the parts of
Libya about Cyrene, and strangers of Rome, Jews
and Proselytes, Cretes and Arabians, and they tell
us in all these different languages about the wonderful works of God !'

"Some of the people whom the Robber taught
to fight against the truth said, 'Oh, it is, just
because the fellows are drunk.' Then Peter said,
'Ye men of Judæa, let it be known to you that we
are not drunk thus early in the day, but that God
Almighty promised hundreds of years ago by the

mouths of His Prophets that he would pour out His Spirit upon men, and this word of His is to-day fulfilled. God has said that He will judge all men who believe not the wonders that He works; but that all that call upon the name of the Lord shall be saved. Jesus of Nazareth, the Son of the Great King, has lived on earth, and God has testified to His Son by making Him work miracles, and live a holy life, and die upon the Cross as the prophets were taught of God to say He should. You crucified Him with your wicked hands, but God has raised Him from the dead, and we are all witnesses of it.'

" Then he read to them from their own Scriptures, and shewed how their kings and prophets had looked for the Saviour, and had known that He must die and rise again, and he made it all as clear to them as if God Himself had spoken; and as he was finishing, he said, 'Let all the people know for a certainty that the great God hath made this Jesus whom you have crucified, the Lord of all, and the Anointed King.'

" When the crowd heard this, they were struck in their consciences, and very much afraid of the anger of God. They whispered to one another and said, 'Men and brethren, what shall we do?'

" Peter heard their words, and said to them,

'Be very sorry for your sins, confess them, and be baptised in the name of the Lord Jesus, and you shall also receive the gift of the Holy Ghost. For the promise of the loving God is even for you, and your children, and all men ever so far off. There is forgiveness for all, and help for all, and heaven for all, even for as many as ever the Lord our God shall call.'

"Great numbers came to the preachers when they heard these glad words, and said they would forsake their sins, and three thousand were baptized that day, and lived true to their faith, worshipping and serving God all their lives long. And the poor friends of Jesus became great Apostles, to save souls, from the hour that the Holy Ghost came upon them. They were gifted with learning and eloquence, whenever they spoke, the hearts of men opened to receive their teaching, and they no longer thought of themselves at all, but only longed to bring souls to God.

"But the wiser they grew the more they loved to pray, and so Peter and John were going into the Temple to pray, when a poor afflicted beggar cried to them for an alms. He was a wretched cripple, and had been all his life, and he lay at the Church door, and begged for his daily bread. But Peter and John said, 'We have no money at all, but the one treasure we have, we are willing to share with you, In the name of Jesus Christ of Nazareth, rise up and walk.' Then Peter took him by the hand, and he stood up, and walked, and ran, and leaped, singing and praising God.

"Numbers of people saw this, and when the Apostles came out of the Church, there was a great multitude gathered together to see the cured cripple. So St. Peter said to them, ' Why are you so astonished at this? The God of your fathers has raised up His Son Jesus, whom you hated and denied, and called out that He should be crucified, and you did crucify Him, but God raised Him from the dead, and glorified Him before you all, so that the power of His name has cured this cripple before your eyes. But, brethren, I know that you did this sin in ignorance, so I entreat you to repent, and be converted, that the sin may be forgiven. Jesus was raised from the dead to ensure forgiveness to all, and He will come again to reward them that serve Him, and punish the impenitent.'

"Many of the poor people who heard this, became very sorry for what they had done against Jesus, and came confessing their sins, and asking for baptism, but the rulers were angry, and seized Peter and John, and brought them before the High Priest.

" You would imagine that these men, who were so frightened when their Master, the Prince, was seized, would have fainted with fear when their own turn came, but no, they were bold as lions, and no thought of fear came near them. What had made such a change in them do you think? Ah, it was the Spirit of God that had changed them from timid children into brave soldiers of Jesus.

" The Chief Priest questioned them as he had questioned Jesus. The work of Jesus was to suffer, and shew patience, and meekness, and silent courage, but the work given to the Apostles, was to make Jesus known, that souls might fly to Him and be saved. The Holy Spirit showed the Apostles what their work was, and taught them what to say and do. So when the High Priest asked them about the cripple, Peter said, " Be it known unto you all, that by the power of the name of Jesus of Nazareth, whom you crucified, and whom God raised from the dead, by His power this man is cured. You rulers despised Jesus, but He is become the head of all, and there is no salvation by any name but His.'

" The rulers were awfully angry at Peter for speaking thus before all in the court, for they had taken such pains to conceal the resurrection of

Jesus, and now he was telling it everywhere. But the boldness of Peter and John alarmed them, besides there stood the man who was healed, so, what could they do? After consulting together they took the Apostles into a private room, and said they would imprison them, and even take their lives, if they preached any more, but for the present they might go free.

"Peter and John answered, 'If it be right to obey you rather than God, you can judge. We are certainly bound to speak the things we have heard and seen.'

"The rulers threatened them again, but let them go. Then the Apostles assembled together, with the Blessed Virgin, and some of the new converts, and they praised God, saying, 'Thou art the great God Who hast created all things, and hast glorified Thy Son Jesus, notwithstanding the rage and cruelty of His enemies. And now behold how these rulers threaten, and grant to Thy servant courage to preach Jesus, and confirm our word by stretching out Thy hand to heal, and to do miracles, that Jesus may be glorified and souls saved.'

"After this people came from all the villages round about, bringing with them sick folks, and cripples, and blind, and whenever the Apostles laid

their hands upon them, and said, 'In the name of
the Lord Jesus,' they were cured, and then the
people listened to the story of the life and death
of Jesus, and believed that He was the Son of God,
and their own Saviour, and begged to be baptized
in His name, and they sold all their possessions,
and made themselves poor as He did to be able to
support those who lost their bread by becoming
Christians.

"Of course the rulers were very angry, and they
caught some of the Apostles, and shut them up in
the common prison; but an angel came at night,
and opened the prison doors, and they went out
into the city, and began immediately to preach and
to teach about the Saviour Jesus.

"Then there were two persons, husband and
wife, who came and told a lie to Peter, saying that
they were giving him all the money they had.
And Peter said, 'The money is your own, you are
free to give it, and you are free to keep it, or to
give some and keep some, only speak the truth, for
it is not to me that you give the money, but to the
Holy Ghost for the poor of His.church.' And they
held to their lie, declaring that it was all they had
when it was only half, and they were struck dead
on the spot.

"A very young disciple, called Stephen, was

filled with the Spirit of God like the rest, and he preached to the people, shewing them by the old Scriptures that Jesus was the Son of God, and that they had sinned grievously in killing Him. Then they got into a fury, and threw great stones at him, hitting and bruising him shockingly. But he prayed to God, and his face shone like that of an angel, and he looked up, and said, ' Behold, I see heaven open, and Jesus standing at the right hand of God.' Then he prayed again, ' Lord, lay not this sin to their charge,' and after that he died so peaceably that they said he fell asleep.

"New Apostles were raised up to help the old ones, for there was so much preaching to be done. Paul and Silas were put into prison, and cruelly flogged ; but all the time of their suffering they prayed and sang praises to God, rejoicing that they were sharing the sufferings of Jesus, and offering them up to God in union with His, for His glory and the salvation of souls. It was their one thought how they could bring souls to Jesus, for He had taught them that the greatest pleasure He could have was to welcome souls to heaven.

The kings and rulers became ever more jealous, for the people who worshipped God badly began to worship Him with contrite and loving hearts, and those who worshipped idols turned to God and became Christians, and destroyed their idols; and bad men of all religions rose against the Apostles, and tried to kill them. But the Apostles went all over the world, wherever the roads were known, and gathered up souls everywhere, teaching the love of Jesus, and baptizing thousands in His dear name.

"The rulers raged, and caught one and another of the Apostles, and some they crucified, and some they killed with the sword, and some they plunged into a caldron of boiling oil, and some they threw to wild beasts. And it was not only the Apostles and Priests, but all the Christians were fearfully persecuted, for the Devil was enraged past bearing, and he enraged his own slaves. Christians were killed by thousands. Young girls were devoured by lions in the presence of crowds of men, young boys chopped in pieces before their parents, men and women were killed in all the different ways you can think of, and the Devil thought he would soon destroy the church. But his thought was folly. Jesus had promised to be ever with His church, the Holy Ghost possessed the hearts of the new Christians—they might kill the bodies of the Christians, but they could not kill Jesus and the Holy Ghost. So whenever one Priest was killed, the Holy Ghost entered into the hearts of half-a-dozen more people, so that they became teachers and preachers, and where the common people were martyred, hundreds that had before been pagans believed in Jesus, and confessed His name, receiving baptism, although they knew that it would cost them their lives. And everywhere priests and people, men and women and children were so full of love to Jesus—so full, that is to say, of the Holy Ghost by whom alone we can truly love Jesus—that they were ready at any time to give all they had, even life itself, to win more souls to His love, that He might rejoice in the fruits of His great work.

"This, dear children, is the 'Promise of the Father,' this the glorious inheritance of the Church of God. The Holy Ghost has not grown weaker than He was in those days, the difference is that the hearts of Christians have grown colder. If our hearts would only grow bigger, we could get more of the Holy Ghost into them. You have heard people talk of the Infallibility of the Church; it is too big a word for you to understand, but it means that the Church cannot teach what is wrong. And why cannot the Church teach what is wrong? Have not the Priests, has not the Pope himself, got sin in the heart? Ah, but it neither depends on Priest, nor on Bishop, nor even on the Pope, it is on the Holy Ghost that the Church leans for her sure wisdom, for the Holy Ghost speaks by her.

It is by the power of the Holy Ghost that the Priest can give absolution, that the Bishop can give confirmation, that the Pope and the Councils can teach the true faith to the Church. Jesus said, 'The Holy Ghost shall teach you all things,' and His word is as true to-day as when the first miracle of the Holy Ghost was worked in the upper chamber at Jerusalem, where timid men were filled with courage, and ignorant ones with wisdom.

" Dear children, we here assembled are poor and insignificant people, and only our good parents and relatives care anything about us. But we are great in one sense, for we are inheritors of the gifts of the Holy Ghost. He dwells in our Church, the Catholic Church, He comes to us, poor and low as we are, when we receive absolution, He enters our hearts when we receive confirmation, and He never leaves us entirely, except we commit mortal sin. But we must love Him and welcome Him, and ask His help, and seek His light, if we want Him to like His home in us. If we do this He will work as of old, by little and little He will teach us zeal for souls, and He will find means for us, notwithstanding our lowness, to work for the salvation of others, so that we shall be a little bit like the old

Christians, who were quite taken up with gathering the harvest for Jesus. In one way we can begin this very night to work with our ever present Lord for the salvation of those he died to save—we can pray for them. Say but a few words with an earnest and loving heart, and some fruit must come of it,—say, 'I offer the blood of Jesus, in union with His love, for the salvation of all in this village.' Do this, and you will be doing Pentecost work, labouring side by side, as it were, with the Holy Ghost at the Christians' never-ending trade of bringing souls to God.

"While we say the decade of the Descent of the Holy Spirit, let us pray for all in this country, and for sinners all over the world."

STORY OF THE FOURTEENTH BEAD.

FILIAL LOVE TO MARY.

"AND so your picture has come round at last, Polly," exclaimed Jack, as the children examined their pictures before the opening of the class; "it looks as nice a picture as a girl could have, I could have wished for it for our Katy, it looks so kind and peaceful like."

"It is very pretty," said Polly, "our Lady going up into heaven, it is; but I doubt the story about it will be difficult."

"They are all difficult to do," said Minnie, "ne'er a one of them easy; only the last seemed to me hardest of all. To be put in prison, and killed so cruelly; oh! I should never have dared to belong to Jesus in those days!"

"The Holy Ghost would have made it all right for you, I'll be bound," said Johnny, with his

knowing nod, " you know it was along of Him that
Peter and the others were such stunning fine
fellows; they were all frightened enough beforehand, just as we are when the ventilator breaks in
the pit. My! don't we run!"

"Run? I should think we do! Why, lad, it's
life and death we run for! if we don't get to the
air in time, the choke damp would be upon us!"
exclaimed Jack; "we should be fools if we didn't
run."

"Supposing the Lord Jesus was there and
couldn't run," whispered Katy.

The suggestion was too perplexing, and no one
spoke for some seconds, then Jack said solemnly:

" It is to be hoped that the Holy Ghost would
give us pluck to pull Him along or to stop and die
with Him."

" I wonder if the Blessed Virgin was frightened
too, before the Holy Ghost came?" said Minnie.

" No, no," said Jack, "the lady never said a
word about her being frightened, she was beside
the cross, and at the burial—always holding up
other people's hearts. It is odd, for women mostly
cries, and faints, and goes on anyhow."

"Why don't you know?" said Tom, "the
Scriptures on Christmas day said as the Holy Ghost
came to her before our Lord was born, and you

know she did no sin, so He was never driven away. That is how her heart kept up."

" Well done, Tom, for a good reason !" cried Jack.

At this moment, Christine sprang into the room, having left her aunt in the school. " I know something," she exclaimed, " Oh, what would you give for my secret ?"

"Tell it to us, Miss Christine, dear, do now," pleaded the children, one and all, and Christine looking very important, said :

" It is papa, and Father Rogers, and Auntie, that I heard talking. Those wild boys who hurt Harry, three of them, I mean, it's about them."

"I believe they are taken to prison for stealing coal," said Tom, looking more proud of his own cleverness than sorry for the sin he imagined.

" Shame, Tom. They have been as regular at Chapel as ourselves, this good bit, they sit near father, and he says they behave first rate."

"They have been baptized," cried Christine. " It is to be kept secret till the Priest can get them taught their religion thoroughly, and then they are to be confirmed. After that," he says, "it may be made known, for the Holy Ghost will give them strength and courage to bear the bullying of the bad boys."

" Hurrah !" cried Jack. The cry was infectious, and when the lady entered the room, all her class were standing, waving hats, handkerchiefs, pictures, or rosaries, or anything else they could get hold of, and shouting with all their might. They subsided into quietness immediately. She reproved Christine for telling what the Priest wanted to remain unknown, and said the Rosary children must promise to pay for their knowledge, by praying daily for the three boys.

" Katy and me has prayed ever since you spoke of it before, ma'am," said Jack.

" Then you've been the first to do Holy Ghost work," said Minnie.

" Not the first, is it, ma'am?" asked Ethel. " Master Harry began this with his kindness and patience. Surely he was the first to do Holy Ghost work to these boys."

" Yes, he certainly began it, Ethel. And when the doctor forgave the injuries, and returned good for evil, he helped it on, and the Priest preaching about Jesus, as Saint Peter and Saint John did so long ago by the teaching of the same Holy Ghost, and the children praying—all this has been like a chain of God's loving mercy, drawing these poor boys to the arms of His dear Son. There is one thing more we can do to help them, another link in God's chain of mercy. We can ask her to pray for them who loves all poor sinners with a mother's heart, the sweet and blessed Virgin."

"Please, ma'am, the picture is mine; can we have the story?" said Polly, rather impatiently.

The big Rosary was placed on the table, and the Fourteenth Bead's story began.

"When Jesus was dying on the Cross, His Mother stood beside Him. She was homeless and friendless, her husband was dead, and she had no one belonging to her, but that dear Son who was at once her child and her God, her Son, and her Saviour, and He was dying too. Rough people were about her, the soldiers with their sharp weapons stood near, threatening, the brutal, ignorant mob jeered and hooted, there was everything to scare and terrify a weak woman, but Mary could endure all rather than leave her dying Son. He in His agony looked down fondly upon her, and saw her breaking heart, and forgot His own griefs to pity hers. One of His disciples was also there, the dearest, and most loving one, and he had a home. So Jesus gave His Mother to him, and thus secured her protection after His death.

"What Jesus said to John, He said through Him to all the Church of God. To the Apostles themselves, to all the early Christians, to every one, who

by the grace of God, is a child of God's Church,—
to them, and to us He says, 'Behold thy Mother.'
He gives her to us to love and sympathise with,
that she may be a guide to us in our way to
heaven.

"Mary lived with her Son's dearest friend, and
with him she attended the constant worship in the
upper chamber. She consoled His sorrow, she
cheered His fainting heart, she urged each and
every one to hope and wait for the promise of the
Father.

"The Holy Ghost descended, and forthwith the
friends of Jesus were changed from a little flock of
timid sheep, into a vast army of bold soldiers, and
the blessed Mother moved among them, sympathi-
zing, praying, soothing, comforting, and doing all
that the most perfect of women could do. She
did not sit down to mourn the absence of her Son,
though He was such a son as never woman had
before, nor ever will have again, but she staid
doing all that she knew He would wish to be done,
and waiting to go to Him till the time that He
thought best.

"For twelve years she waited, ever busy with
acts of courage, and zeal, and humility, and love.
And then He called her to Him. She loved to die
as He had died, and meekly yielding her spirit into

His loved hands, she ended her mortal life, at the age of about sixty years.

"And the heavens opened, and choirs of angels descended, and took her in their arms, and carried her upwards, and at heaven's gate Jesus received her. The separation was over, the partings were finished—the handmaid of the Lord was at rest for ever in the arms of her divine Son. 'Behold thy Mother,' Jesus still says, for though Mary is at rest, and glorified, she is more than ever our Mother. She still loves our sympathy, and if we desire to please Jesus our best plan is to imitate His Mother, for who had learned the art of pleasing Him half so well as she had?

"First then, dear children, let us cultivate a tender sympathy for Mary, in her sorrows and in her joys.

"From the time that the Angel found her in her quiet humble home, one grief after another came upon her. First, there was the trial of homelessness and poverty—what mother would not grieve at having no better cradle for her child than a manger, no snug fireside, no comfortable bed—only straw and rough walls and the beasts all around her. When the holy child came Mary loved Him with intense devotion, and treasured Him most dearly; but when first she took Him to the Temple, to present Him to the Lord, the aged Prophet told her that for her child's sake, ' a sword should pierce through her own soul.' The Shepherds adored Him, the Wise Men came from their far country to worship at His feet, yet the Holy Family continued poor, and Mary watched her child, and pondered in her heart all that the Prophet and the Wise Men said about Him.

, "Soon her cares began to increase ; an angel came by night to Joseph, and said that the governor was trying to take the young child's life, and they must fly with Him to Egypt. So Mary and Joseph took a long journey in fear and anxiety. Mary rode on an ass, and carried her precious child in her arms, and Joseph walked beside them. The heat made their way trying, robbers beset them, and they had many a grief ; but they reached Egypt in safety, and were there till the time of the death of the cruel persecutors.

"When Mary thought she had lost her dear Son when they were returning to Nazareth after He had first assisted at the Sacrifices in the Temple, then there was another sword-stab in her heart. Indeed all her sorrows were for her Son, she had no thoughts for herself ; during her whole life we never hear of one act of selfishness, or of any leaning toward such an act.

"She suffered most of the things that other women are called upon to suffer—she lost her husband, she lost her home, her Son left her to preach and teach, to heal the sick, and cast out devils, in fact, 'to do His Father's business.' Mary only saw him occasionally—the only time she asked Him to do a miracle it was out of consideration for others : they were at a marriage feast, the master had no more wine, and she asked her Son to supply some for them. He did as she wished, but said His time had not yet come, the time when He would grant blessings in full measure at her request.

"Who can avoid pitying that afflicted Mother at the time of Christ's Passion. All the devotion of the best women was centred in her heart for the Son whom she loved was infinitely more lovable than the best sons of the human race. If any other mother longs for the success of her child, longs to see him honoured, loved, and admired, how much more might she, but instead of love, He received hatred instead of honour, contempt instead of a throne, a Cross of Shame instead of gifts, reproach and insults. He had been so busy saving souls, and giving all directions to His disciples for founding and governing, strengthening and enlarging His Church, that for some time He had not seen His Mother. A terrible report reached her ears ; her

Son was taken prisoner, and brought before the Judge, and the people were crying out that He should be crucified. How the sword pierced her heart when she heard those words; but it was worse when she met Him on the way to Calvary, wearily carrying His Cross, His face marred with suffering, and with blood, and His strength well nigh exhausted.

"Nor were her sufferings less when she stood beside the Cross to witness His death of agony. Were it not for the Holy Ghost dwelling in her, giving her Divine help and strength, her woman's heart must then have broken. But her faith never wavered ; she did not consider all was lost as the disciples did, and she laid her Beloved One in the tomb, sure that somehow or other he would make His every promise good by conquering death and redeeming His people. How and when He would do it she did not know ; but in her deepest sorrow her will was still one with that of her Lord, and the language of her heart still was 'Behold the handmaid of the Lord; let him do with me just what He pleases.' She longed for the presence of her dear Son more than any earthly woman can long for her entirely human treasure, yet she was willing to wait just as long as He thought good ere she went to Him.

"And Mary had her joys also. She was glad when the Shepherds adored Him, when the Wise Men came to pay Him homage, when the Prophet recognised Him as the expected Messias, and when the people received Him as their Lord and Saviour. But she was more glad when after those days of darkness and solitude, Jesus stood before her on the Resurrection morning, and told her that His Passion was ended, and His triumph begun. Her heart thrilled with joy when He stood among His little band of loved ones in the upper chamber, and said, 'Peace be unto you.' She was glad at heart when the Holy Ghost descended, and the Apostles received the power, as they had already received the commission, to teach and to preach, and when the power of Jesus was manifested by the conversion of thousands in one day. But when her call came, and her long pilgrimage ended, she entered into the house of her Son and Lord, then more than ever did her spirit rejoice in God her Saviour, who by His greatness had exalted her, of all the human race the most humble and the most meek.

"It is because of all these things that we love to say the Hail Mary, as if we were to say, 'Sweet Mother, we feel with you in your sorrows, and are glad in your joy. Jesus is the King and Lord of our hearts, we live only by Him, we want to love whom He loves, and you first as ever nearest and dearest to His heart. Hail, Mary, full of grace, the Lord is with thee! We congratulate you that all separation is over, and you dwell for ever with Him. You are holy, you are the true Mother of Jesus, be kind and compassionate to your poor children on earth, who are always in need, always in danger, and most in both at the dread hour of death. You have died, and Joseph has died, pity the dying. Holy Mary, Mother of God, pray for us sinners, now, and at the hour of our death.'

" In the present day the Devil is very busy putting bad books into people's hands. People have got very fond of reading, and listening to stories, and the Devil makes use of this to fill their minds with evil. Priests, and teachers, and masters, and all who have to do with young people, know how much harm is done by these exciting stories. Men and women are described as handsome, or clever, cunning, or daring—any way to make people think very much of them, and keep constantly looking at the picture of them in their own minds. These imaginary people do wicked actions, but they do them so cleverly, that they make them look pleasant instead of disgusting, and the young people who read it all think about it till they are attracted to do the same bad actions.

" Now we tell you about the Blessed Virgin on purpose to put quite a contrary kind of picture into your mind. She is made the most glorious of created beings, just because she was humble, and loving, and obedient, and thought of nothing else but just to do the will of God. The fine ladies in the romances are made to say and do all sorts of grand things, and silly boys and girls long to say and do like them. But first they must know that all those things are lies, and no one ever did them, and secondly that the honours and glories they pretended to get were over in a very short time. On the other hand the humility and unselfishness of the Blessed Virgin are simply described by the pen of the Holy Ghost ; and the reward that Jesus gave to her, and promises to us, if we practise her virtues, and love Him as she did, is sure as the truth of God.

" Let us say the decade in tender sympathy with all the joys and sorrows of our Lady, and praying for such a likeness to her, and love of her, as shall help us to please Our Lord."

STORY OF THE FIFTEENTH BEAD.

PERSEVERANCE TO THE END.

" OW it is my picture," cried little Pat. " Mother has been keeping it safe till to-day ; see how pretty the beautiful lady is with the crown on her head, and all the children a singing about her. Isn't it nice, Janey ?"

" It isn't nicer than our chapel was on Christmas morning, Patsy, when it was all dark and cold outside, and the chapel was bright as day, with such lots and loads of candles, and the flowers, and the beautiful writings everywhere, and the boys singing so loud and beautiful. I wish Christmas Day would come every week !"

" There is one wish !" exclaimed the teacher, who had entered unobserved. " Now let me hear what some one else would like. What would your choice be, Minnie ?'

" Oh I would have a pic-nic once a week, such as we had in the summer on Machen mountain. We were right away at the top there, and we could see the sea and the ships on it, and the castle on the cliff, and our village down here just like one of Miss Christine's toys, and there was no smoke about us, but plenty of flowers, and we ran where-ever we liked, and sang all our hymns as loud as we could, to make sure that God would hear them. Oh, but wasn't it nice !"

" I liked the concert best, ma'am," said Ethel, gently ; " the music seemed to make one glad and sorry at the same time. But when all sung toge-ther, and I knew the words, oh then it was beauti-ful, quite ! If I might have my wish, it should be a concert once a week."

" It wouldn't be my wish," said Ellen Sullivan. " The music is nice, but when they sang 'Father come home,' it made poor mother and me cry fit to break our hearts, for it minded us of Father who never can come home again."

" But suppose, Ellen, your father had come when you called him ?"

" Oh, then I should have loved the concert better than anything, just for bringing him !"

" Then your wish would be to have your father back ?"

" Oh yes, ma'am, that would be the grandest thing for both mother and us !"

" And I would wish for Harry !" whispered Christine.

" And I for little Dan," added Katy.

" And what would the boys have ?" asked the lady. " Mind it must be something certainly not sinful."

" Could it be a good long ride on a merry-go-round in a fair, ma'am ?" asked Johnny.

" Wouldn't a horse along the moor do as well, Johnny ?"

" Every bit as well, ma'am, only it is out of the reach of us lads."

" Just so. I object to the fair, because its pleasures are generally mingled with bad language, cheating, and intemperance. A good long ride over the hills would be as cheery and quite harm-less. You know we are only playing at wishes."

" Well, then, I'll wish for plenty of jolly rides."

" And I would like a holiday to the town, with Katy by the hand, and father and mother to see the shops too, and enough of victuals with us," said Jack.

" I would have a good sail on the sea. It is so nice to see the water splashing against the boat, and to feel the wind blowing in your face, and the ship

14

going on ever so fast—oh I do like to be on the sea, it seems so free and careless-like—no school-bell and works'-bell, nothing to stop one's pleasure. I will choose a day on the sea." Such was Tom's decision.

"I would play with those nice little girls, who came to aunt's last year," said Eleanor; "they were nicer mannered than we are here, and so kind, and they taught me new games, and new tunes, and were never cross or vexed with one. Oh they were darlings!"

"I would be so as one couldn't be hungry, or cold, or vexed," said Timothy, "and neither father nor mother should have to work. If it isn't too much I would wish for us all to have a good long rest, and no want of victuals."

"Well now, children, let us hear the Fifteenth Bead's story, and see what Holy Mary got, who never wished at all, but left everything good to be chosen for her by her beloved Son. During the sixty years of her mortal life she had known plenty about hunger, and cold, and homelessness, and sorrow, and pain, and the loss of all nearest and dearest to her; and she had endured in full measure that keenest of all suffering, the sight of the agony of her Best-beloved. The Robber-king had tried every means to turn aside the stedfast heart

of the handmaid of the Lord, but in every moment
of trial she had persevered in keeping her eyes
upon her Son and Saviour, and His help had been
every ready for her need. In darkness and dreariness, in sorrow and temptation her Faith, Hope,
and Love had never failed ; she had waited the
King's own time for bestowing upon her the reward
of her humility and weakness, and her reward was
all the surer for the waiting.

"And now the day is come when Mary's griefs
are ended and her joys perfected. She dies as
Jesus died, commending her spirit into the Father's
hands, and falling asleep in Jesus, awakes to glory.
Carried at once to the Palace of her Son, to share
its rejoicings, her happiness cannot be perfect while
her body is in the prison house of the tomb. The
soul can rest, and enjoy, and glorify God in His dear
presence, even while the body waits in the grave
for the Resurrection Day ; but the happiness is not
full and entire until the body too is saved and
glorified in heaven. The death of the body and its
continuance in the grave is the penance due to sin,
the guilt of which is atoned by the Sacrifice of
Jesus. Mary died though sinless, willing to share
the lot of her children, in this meek obedience to
death, as she had been willing to wash her soul
according to the law, though no stain had fallen

14—2

on it, and God accepted this last act of sweet obedience, but would not let the body that had con-
tained His Son moulder in the grave, so the angels
fetched it to heaven, to rejoin the soul, and all
the heavenly choirs sang, 'Alleluia. Glory to
God.'

"Then the Prince of Peace led her to her seat at
his · right hand, and he placed upon her head a
glorious crown, the jewels of which shone so
brightly that even the angels could scarcely bear to
look upon them. Mary had forgotten her own
acts of humility, and love, and obedience, for she
had had no thoughts to spare for anything but
the noble deeds of her Son, and the necessities of
his poor servants; but while her heart was busy
with him, he had guarded all her jewels for her,
and made them a hundred times more beautiful and
bright by keeping them with his own.

" The Father smiled, and bent downwards in love
and tenderness to His dearest daughter, and the
Holy Spirit nestled to her heart as Jesus embraced
his mother, and placing the crown upon her head,
hailed her Queen of Heaven. Then every harp in
heaven was attuned to softest strains, and every
angelic voice gave forth its fullest harmony, and the
triumphant song of the angels was echoed by the
grateful gladness of the saints — ' Hail, Mary,

Queen of Heaven.' The angels and archangels, and the spirits of the just, did homage to their Queen, and all the time she saw nothing but the dazzling glory of her Son, desired nothing but to do his most dear will, and her heart's reply still was 'Behold the handmaid of the Lord; be it unto me according to thy word.'

"Thus, children, our generous Saviour would bestow yet another gift upon His family on earth. Mary must reign in heaven, not only as a reward for her poverty and self-sacrifice on earth, but as a help and favour to her children, who still have to carry on the warfare with the Robber on earth. You know that when a town gets very full of people, and so of considerable importance, it is allowed to choose a member to sit in parliament, and help to govern the kingdom, so that if any wrong were done to that town, her representative, as the member is called, might tell all her wrongs to the government, and secure justice being done to her.   Now just in this sense Mary is our representative beside the throne of God; she loves and pities us, and is ever ready to take our part.   She has no difficult part to act, nothing that can weary or fret her, for when she turns to plead for us with Jesus, He is loving us already, and only waiting for some excuse to give all that is asked.

But as He sits there on His glorious throne, waiting till every enemy is destroyed, He sits as a Judge. God has committed all judgment into His hands, that is why we are so thankful for Mary as an Advocate. It is He who will pronounce our sentence, He whom we have seen as the Child of Bethlehem, the Man of Sorrows, the Cross-bearer, the Lamb slain has begun his work of judgment, and at his bar we must each stand for our trial. Accusers we have in abundance, Satan and his demons keep a register of our sins—there is no honour in their black hearts, they will not pity us because they tempted us to the sins, but they will eagerly demand our damnation on account of them. Our Angel Guardian will try to defend, Mary will plead for us, but only when the Judge sees that our claims to His purchased pardon and righteousness are just will He pronounce the blessed words of acquittal. He has borne all the punishment for us, but we must be united to Him by our own free choice, and persevere in that union, if we would be justified at our trial.

"Thus we come to the crowning Virtue of Perseverance, the most difficult of all, and the most necessary. For this we must pray all our lives long, for Jesus will only give it to us day by day, like our daily bread. It is the will of God that we depend continually upon Him, and so He will only give us what is necessary at the time.. For to-morrow's need to-morrow's grace is ready ; His store never falls short, but it will be given in answer to to-morrow's prayer.

"In Holy Scripture we read of some who followed Christ for a time, because they saw his miracles, but were offended at something He said, which they could not understand, and so they went away from Him. They perished for want of the grace of Perseverance, Others again followed the Apostles in the same way, but turned from Jesus again because they loved the present evil world. They also were lost for want of perseverance.

"Nothing on earth can be done without perse-verance, how then could he reasonably expect to gain heaven without it. A child has to learn reading by perseverance—it is not one day's lesson, but daily lessons of weeks and months, and some-times even years. You learn men's work in the same way ; many trades take seven years to learn. If you gave up towards the end of the time, all would be wasted. So it is with the trade of sav-ing one's soul. }

. "Before we say the decade in honour of the Coronation of the Blessed Virgin to implore the grace of Perseverance, I will tell you a dream or vision, to help you to understand the great joy that you may each reach by perseverance.

"There was a town on fire, and many of the inhabitants were burnt to death; but a number of young lads and girls escaped, and ran away across the country, not knowing where they went. A youth met them, clothed in white, and he said, 'If you want to escape all evils, climb to the top of that mountain, and you will find the best possible country; but it is a hard mountain to climb, and you may be years in getting to the top;' and having said that, he went on his way.

"The pilgrims soon came to the foot of the mountain, and began the ascent.

"There were numerous trees and bushes growing on the lower part of the mountain, so that for miles it was like a forest, and they could not see the road before them, nor know whether they were losing their way or not; only the thoughtful ones were sure that as they were trying to get to the top of the mountain, they could only be right when climbing upwards; but many of the others argued that this was not the case, and turned to the right and the left, and made homes in the forest, not knowing that the fire was spreading on towards it. Several of the party never emerged at all from the forest, and many more tarried there a long time, so

it was only half the party that went on immediately, and many of these were grumbling because
they could not rest longer.

"Beyond the forest the road was steep and
rocky, and they cut their feet, and, often falling,
bruised themselves sadly; and then some said it
was hard to have to be pilgrims, and those were
well off who had staid in the forest, and some
even went back. But the thoughtful ones said,
'Danger is behind, safety before; the best land is
worth some pain in reaching it.'

"Then they came to a place where vines grew,
and there were plenty of grapes, and they ate of
these and were refreshed, and took some with them
to refresh themselves in time of need; also they
were able to buy bread. So some said, 'This is
a good enough land, we will stay here,' and they
went no further. Of those that persevered after
this, two or three lost heart when the bread and
grapes were done; hunger, they said, was a bad
companion, so they turned back to the vineyard.

"The next difficulty was a steep slope all covered
with thorns and brambles. It cost many a pain to
traverse this, and it was not all who had courage
to do it. Their feet were torn and wounded, and
their clothes sadly injured; indeed, they were so
lame when they got to the other side, that they

were forced to sit down and rest, though the sun was terribly scorching. And they saw that many had turned back, and were going to the right and the left, and seeking where to live.

" At last they came to a steep precipice, and there was no other way upwards, only paths to the right and the left winding round the mountain. They were in great perplexity, for only about twenty remained, and these were all of different minds ; some wanted to go to the right, some to the left, and only three or four had the boldness to think of climbing the precipice. A smiling guide appeared, and said, ' Come to the right, friends, and I will lead you by slow degrees to the mountain top ;' and ere he had done speaking another came, and said, ' Do not follow him, the road to the left is better ; come my way, and I will lead you through a tunnel to the mountain top.'

" Then they disputed hotly together which way was best, and they quarrelled and fought with one another, and then six went indignantly off to the right, saying to the rest, ' You deserve never to reach the good land for your stupidity ;' and six went to the left, saying, ' Nay, it is you who are stupid,' and eight remained standing in uncertainty, and they cried aloud, ' Oh for a true guide to lead us to the mountain top !' and when they had cried thus, the white guide came to them whom they had seen in the plain, and he shewed them little holes in the rock, into which they could put their feet, and he gave them each two grappling irons, by which they could cling to the rock, and he said, 'Take these irons, patience and perseverance, and climb up with them, and you will find the good land.' And so they climbed, until first one and then another, and finally all the eight entered the Good Land.

"As soon as they entered they heard a song of welcome on every side, and white-robed creatures came to them to give them all that they could need. They took them to a bath, and washed them so that they were quite clean, and as soon as they dipped in the water all their scratches and bruises were healed, and all the aching was taken out of their bones.

"When they came from the bath clean soft clothing was given to them, and they gazed one at another in astonishment, for what with the bath, and what with the beautiful white raiment, each looked fair and handsome, and young, and healthy, every one like the son or the daughter of a queen. They had felt very hungry before going to the bath, but now it seemed to them as if they had eaten good food, and were satisfied ; they remarked to the attendants that it was pleasant to be free from the pain of hunger and thirst, and they smiled kindly and said, 'Ah, they never come here—you have done with them.'

They were next taken to the King, and he welcomed them too, and the King's Son gave them papers which were the title deeds of lands and houses, so that each should have a good home of his own. And the Prince's mother smiled on them, and bade them welcome, and told them to come to her whenever they liked, for she would always be a mother to them, and as she spoke she looked so sweet and loving, that they determined to go to her very often. All over the country there were fields and gardens and fruit trees in abundance, and you could take the fruit whenever you pleased, for there was enough for all, and some of the trees ripened their fruit every month. No weeds grew, and the land never wanted digging, for the trees and corn grew just as the King told them without needing any work.

"When the pilgrims went to their homes they did not find them empty. One was met in the doorway by father and mother, who had died in the time of the famine, but they had been resting since, and now had got possession of the good home. Another found little brothers, and sisters, and companions ; another uncles, and aunts, and kind friends who had gone before. And all that were there were dressed in white, and looked fresh and beautiful, and not one of their bad habits remained, but they were all love and gladness, and had a never ending story to tell of the goodness and generosity of the King.

"The pilgrims sat in the summer evenings under the pleasant trees, surrounded by loving relations, and old friends, or sweet new acquaintances, and they told the story of their pilgrimage, and of those who had turned aside and left them, and the others had similar stories to tell, for most had made the same pilgrimage, though a few had come quickly through the air, some on the white wings of innocence, and some over the tree tops on the blood-red wings of martyrdom. When they recounted their dangers, and heard of those of their friends, they said, 'Glory be to the King for saving us from all.'

"As soon as this word had passed their lips, a golden harp was put into every hand, and they began to play a triumphant air, and to sing, 'Alleluia, salvation and honour, and glory, and power unto the Lord our King!' They sang this over and over again, and when they stopped another group of white robed-creatures, at some distance took up the song 'Alleluia, salvation and honour, and glory, and power, unto the Lord our King, and as they finished another and another company took it up, so that the song was sung every bit over the land, and sometimes all sang together, so that the sound was like the flowing of a mighty torrent, as the whole nation chaunted in one voice, 'Alleluia, salvation and honour and glory, and power unto the Lord our King.'

"They were not always singing, for that would have become wearisome. Sometimes the King sent them on messages, to call some of the loiterers from the forest or the vineyard on the mountain side. They were very glad when these messages were given them, for it was delightful to serve the King, whom they loved so dearly, and when they spread out their grand wings to fly, it was like riding on the swiftest horse, and they could go faster than any railway train. Most days they had messages to do, or were called to assist in the Palace, and it was hard to say which was the greatest treat, to look upon the King, and hear his voice, or to fly on his errands. Whatever they did, and wherever they went, the moment their work was done they began to sing again, so that always in that good land you could hear the sweetest concert that was ever heard, for the golden harps had never done their accompaniment to the 'Alleluia' of the Redeemed.

" Such, dear children, is the Good Land which Adam and Eve lost by disobedience, and Jesus won back by His life of holiness, and death of agony. Jesus invites us each to enter into union with Him by confessing and forsaking our sins, and if we cling to Him by constant love and prayer, He will help us on by little and little, giving us one virtue after another, one grace to crown another, till at last He perfects His work in us by the gift of perseverance. Not only to-day but every day let us pray for this grace, asking our Blessed Mother to join her intercession with our prayers to procure it for us.

" You have now learned all the Mysteries of the Rosary, and can begin the prayers of the Circle. For this month you must each pin your picture beside your bed, and ere you go to rest say the decade belonging to the picture, praying that all the others of the Circle may receive the same grace that you ask for yourself, and offering their actions as well as your own in union with those of Jesus. Thus the whole Rosary will be said among you each night, and each of you will gain as many graces and blessings as if you had said the whole yourself.

" Next month a new set of pictures will be given out, and each will have a different Mystery to that he now has."

" Please ma'am our Bill and Ned will soon be able

to learn the Rosary, and the little Conollys are coming on and them new lads will be getting confirmed."

"True, Timothy, we shall have to think about a second Circle before long ; indeed if you fifteen pray faithfully for your neighbours, I shall not despair of our getting up even a third Circle. But all depends on Perseverance, things are easy in the beginning, but we can't keep on at any good thing except by daily praying for the help of God."

FINIS.